WILL INK SUFFICE?

WILL INK SUFFICE?

ALEXANDER HOMOC

✱ **green**hill

https://greenhillpublishing.com.au/

Homoc, Alexander (author)
Will Ink Suffice?
ISBN 978-1-923088-23-8
FICTION | HISTORY | ROMANCE

Typeset 10/14
Cover Design by Bailey Parrôt
Book design by Green Hill

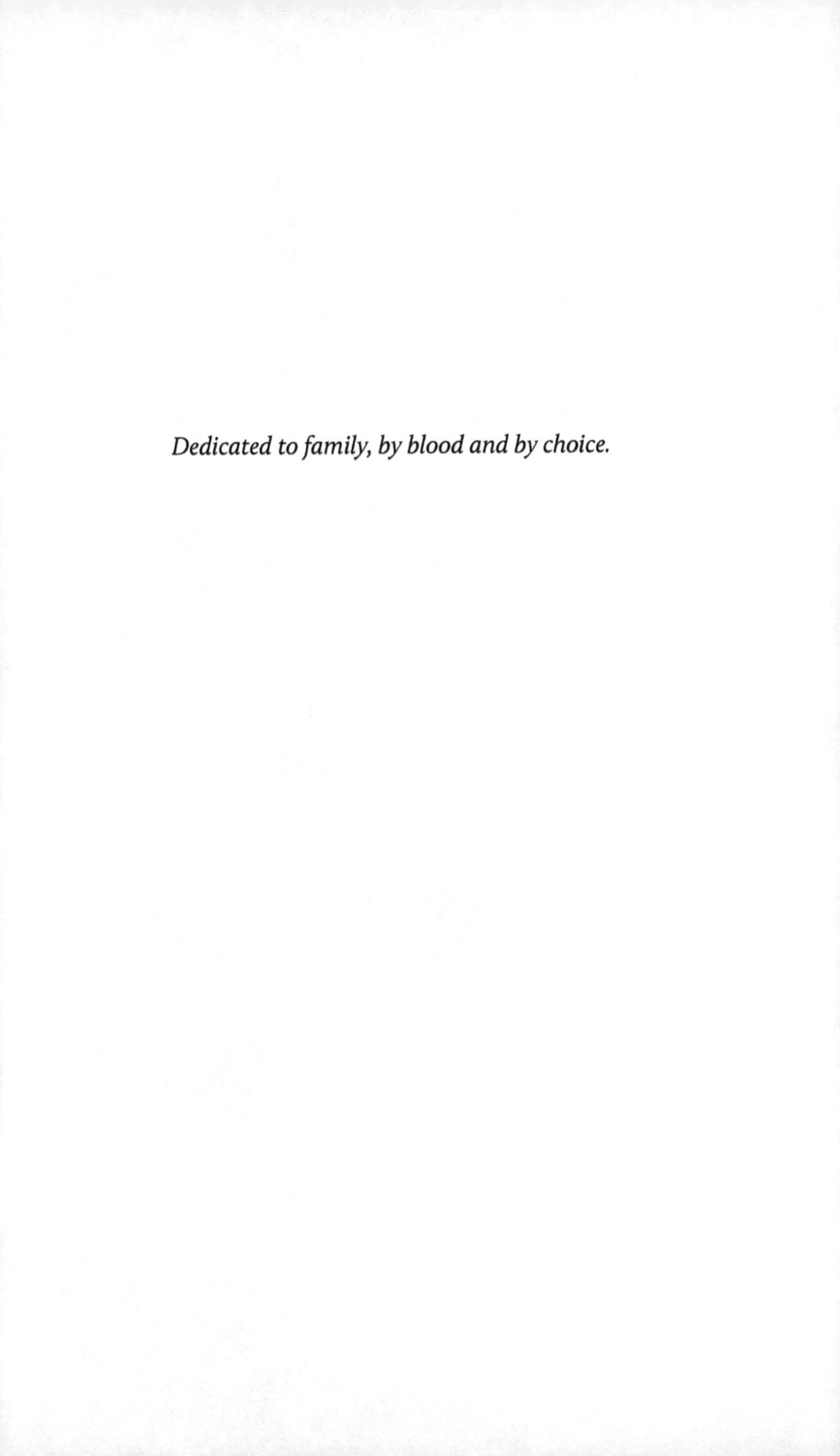

Dedicated to family, by blood and by choice.

CHAPTER ONE

VIVIENNE—IT MEANS ALIVE. Her mother named her after only ever bearing one child. Following three miscarriages and a stillbirth, Vivienne was Marion's miracle baby. Marion was a petite lady, elegant and strong willed. Not elegant in a snobbish way, but in the sense that the shade of her shoes and dress always complemented each other impeccably. An innate elegance that couldn't be taught or bought. Marion owned a quaint bookstore on the outskirts of Montreuil, which had been in their family for over one hundred and seventy-five years and was one of the oldest operating bookstores in the area. Vivienne's father was an architect. He was a man of very few words, or perhaps he could never fit in a word with Marion's lack of an off switch. His presence brought tranquillity and peace to the house in an almost ornamental way.

There was nothing abnormal about her family, nothing that caused neighbours to pry or her peers to whisper. Every evening, they would sit together and enjoy their supper and Marion would enjoy a nice glass of rosé. Well, 'glass' may have been an understatement. Before anyone knew, the entire bottle had been finished and she had stepped onto the coffee table, her youthful cheeks glistening to the sound of some record found lying in a pile of disregarded books. That was another thing about Vivienne: her house was littered with books. Some days, she could barely squeeze through the hallway to arrive at the front door. Probably why she was such an avid reader. It was known—but unspoken—by many of the authority figures in Vivienne's life that she was witty yet stubborn. If Vivienne was a drink, she would have been equal parts of those two potent liquors.

She never had an abundance of friends growing up. Many of the people around her lacked the emotional maturity to keep up with her intense persona. Thomas was that rare exception, like a shooting star or eclipse. Thomas was Vivienne's closest friend, who she considered blood. He was charming, charismatic, and above all, passionate. That's what she respected most about Thomas—he was passionate. Vivienne vividly remembered lying on her bed with Thomas, in the scorching heat, reading a book about love. The books she read—or at least enjoyed—were always about love. He mocked her all afternoon. But in the morning, the book was gone. And then ten days later, it reappeared on her bedside table, unscathed. She knew who the thief was, but how could she hate someone who loved love as much as she did? Even if he hated to admit it. Although the two of them were different in many ways, they were inseparable, their orbit around each other unbreakable. They would ride their bicycles in the rain together, share tubs of yoghurt, and laugh until both were physically unable to speak.

However, fate ended up having unfortunate plans for their friendship. At the age of sixteen, Thomas's father was diagnosed with stage three pancreatic cancer, leaving his mother a soon-to-be widow. Shortly after, the family left France to live with relatives in Canada. Vivienne was distraught. All she had to comfort her was a note that Thomas had left under a ceramic pot on the kitchen table while she slept. It read, *'Dear Vivienne, I'm leaving France and I don't know when I'll return. There is so much I want to say, but I don't know where to begin. I wish I had the courage to say goodbye in person. Thomas.'* She wondered how the world could be so cruel as to take away a person she loved so dearly. This was the first time she'd suffered real pain, but it certainly was not the last.

Over the following years, Vivienne delved into her studies. She was dedicated, her efforts sometimes sporadic, often due to the lack of purpose she felt within her own life. When she thought about the future, she felt nervous and excited and overwhelmed to the point where she thought she might combust. Whenever these intrusive thoughts arose, she would look out her bedroom window and stare into the white-dotted abyss. The vastness of it all provided a sense of relief. At those moments, Vivienne knew she was going to have an impact on the world. Mediocrity was not an option.

From a fairly young age, she knew who she wanted to be. She wanted to be a writer, an author. Not just any author. Vivienne wanted to see her novels in every front window of every bookstore in Paris. She wanted the world to know the name Vivienne LaRue.

As Adrion slammed the door behind him, Vivienne knew a crucial decision had to be made. A decision that would impact her immeasurably.

CHAPTER TWO

Vivienne awkwardly shuffled against the door, both her hands full with the contents of her past. She dropped her bags and ran to the window as the door ricocheted behind her. Although it was not the sixth-storey scenery she imagined it to be, it was still perfect. The apartment wasn't massive. Then again, she was never a fan of unnecessary room. Vivienne walked across the parquetry floorboards and entered the kitchen, which had a kettle and three loose tea bags next to it, courtesies of the owner. They were very grateful when she offered to rent the apartment. Finding a suitable tenant had been a struggle, they said. As she moseyed to the sofa with her tea, a faint voice whispered from the other side of the hall.

'Hello. Vivienne, I presume?' A tall, slender woman announced as she approached the doorway. The woman was fairly attractive, around the same height as Vivienne with perfectly curled blond hair, dressed to the nines in a striking, navy silk dress. Vivienne hastily sat up and walked towards the door.

'Uh—yes, I am.' She hesitated. 'I just moved here.' She was not usually timid, yet the sheer grace of the woman standing before her had caught her off guard.

'Yes, John had mentioned that he'd found someone for the

apartment. Where did you move from?' the woman said, now with one foot in the apartment.

'I lived in Montreuil with my parents. I came to pursue my studies.'

'Why did you move? Montreuil is not that far.'

'No car and I like my independence.' Vivienne broke eye contact with the woman. 'Would have to leave eventually.'

'You make a good point. I just wanted to check in and let you know that if you need anything, I'm just down the hall,' she said with a kind smile.

'Thank you.'

'Also, before I forget, don't leave the window open at night. We have a rodent problem.' The woman raised her voice from the edge of the hall, fading into her apartment. Vivienne took careful note, then returned to her cup of tea, which was now edging lukewarm. It had only just occurred to her that she hadn't managed to catch the woman's name. She wondered how she could simply skim over such an important piece of information. Flustered, maybe? The kettle began to squeal for the second time in the past hour. She allowed the tea to brew in her cup and hauled over one of the boxes that had been dropped off earlier that day. This particular box contained all her favourite books that she had collected over the years. In her assemblage were novels ranging from the classic *King Lear* by William Shakespeare to a book called *The Sleepy Giraffe*. *The Sleepy Giraffe* was a children's story that Vivienne's mother used to read to her before she slept, a night-time ritual that was rarely missed. On the occasions that *The Sleepy Giraffe* was not read, hell would follow. It wasn't the most complex text, but her favourite, and when she read it, she could hear her mother's voice huddled in her ear.

The sun rose and brushed gently against Vivienne's forehead. She slowly woke from her slumber and turned to look at the alarm clock, soon realising that she had yet to unpack it. She hadn't slept with any bed linen that night, but instead under an extremely itchy fur coat she'd found in the closet. The faulty gas heater had stopped working halfway through the night, turning the room bitterly cold. It clicked why possible tenants were reluctant to move in. At least there were no sightings of any mice, gallivanting through the night. Vivienne approached the stove with the kettle and turned it on, then swiftly switched it off, realising that surviving her first morning at university was going to require something stronger. Although the idea of enjoying a shot of cognac at eight o'clock in the morning crossed her mind briefly, she concluded that a double shot of espresso would have been the safer bet.

She began drinking at roughly the age of seventeen. It started with occasionally having a few sips of her mother's wine. By eighteen, a small bottle of whisky was kept under her desk drawer. To say she became a functioning alcoholic in her final year of school might have been a stretch. It just took the edge off—and helped her sleep. Her parents never found out, of course; she was excellent at hiding things, emotions included. Most people had no idea the feelings that ran through her head at any given time. Which was something she inherited from her father, because her mother was an open book. Marion's facial expressions were far from subtle. There *was* one occasion where Vivienne hurled a lamp through her bedroom window during an outburst of pure frustration. Luckily, no one witnessed the event unfold.

Vivienne walked to her room and grabbed her bag, purse, house keys, and lipstick. She generally never used lipstick but assumed that it would come in use at some point. She locked the door to her apartment and was out and down the stairs faster than a hummingbird at the sight of nectar. The morning was crisp. Not unexpected in mid-September. Rue Rene was the street where her apartment was located, and on the corner was a café that she had spotted on the day she moved in. It was petite, with three tables situated in the building and two tables that ran along the exterior. Outside was a burgundy sign that read 'Rene's Patisserie'. The café wasn't anything fancy per se but had an inviting aura that was hard to resist. Vivienne entered, instantly greeted by the intoxicating smell of freshly baked sourdough bread.

'What can I get for you today, darling?' a lady asked, approaching the front counter.

'Could I please get a double shot of espresso, with one extra shot, as well as that right there,' she replied, pointing at an unnamed pastry behind the counter.

Vivienne drew her wrist out of her pocket. The time read quarter past eight, meaning she was on schedule to make her first class. As a matter of fact, she was going to be early, which was unusual.

The woman handed Vivienne her coffee and pastry. 'Here you go, darling.'

'Thank you. Have a nice day.' She took the order, wrapped her scarf around her neck, and exited the shop. Swallowing one large mouthful of the coffee, she analysed the flavours intensely. The initial taste was okay, but it was too bitter. She'd had more luck with instant coffee and made a mental note to buy some. The coffee may not have been fantastic, however the pastry was sensational. Vivienne finished the last few bites and marched up the stone stairs that led to the entrance of the university.

She had been thinking about this moment for several years now, about how accomplished she would feel entering those walls. That was the thing about expectations—they were rarely lived up to. But Vivienne always attained unrealistic expectations, romanticising everything to an impractical point. The university's beauty was no small feat. Filled with arches with fine engravings, domes, and pillars, the architecture was simply astounding. Down the hall were several staff directing students. One of the supervisors pointed Vivienne towards a lecture room where the classes for the semester would take place. She was studying writing and literature, as well as history, which was her elective subject. The room had about eighty fitted seats, and at the front was Professor Clarke—who was yet to look up—and was part of the writing and literature faculty at the university. An extremely accomplished woman who had written several works over her time, ranging from published novels to even writing some of the texts that the university used as part of the syllabus. A few years back, she was invited to teach.

Vivienne sat in the second row from the front, her hand extended to the girl next to her. 'Hi, I'm Vivienne.'

'Mary,' the girl responded as they shook hands.

'Alright, settle down,' Professor Clarke said, standing up from her desk at the front.

'As many of you may know, I'm Professor Clarke. I will be teaching you for the next few years.' She paused. 'Some of you will excel and some of you will not; this is the harsh reality.' She inched closer towards where the students were seated, her wise grey roots staring with conviction. 'Take this class seriously, engage, and above all, be original. *Anyone* can write and speak, but very few can turn those words into something that moves people.' Vivienne looked around the class to see the other students—or, in her mind, the competition. 'Your first assignment will be to write a short essay on any topic regarding this novel.' The laminated blue cover glinted in the professor's hand. 'I picked it randomly from my collection at home. Now, I can't remember exactly what the book is about, I just want to be moved by your writing.' Clarke began to retreat to the board. 'There will be a book for each of you at the front door. If you have any questions, don't be afraid to ask.' Vivienne stood and moved to the back of the room. '*The Seven Castles,*' she murmured to herself as she picked up the slim novel that was no more than a centimetre and a half, which came under her classification of light reading. By the time the class had finished, the pages of the book were riddled with underlined sections and personal annotations.

Her next class was in a room labelled M. Gabriella. She took her seat and allowed her bag to droop from her shoulder to the floor. A man entered, the history teacher, Monsieur Belan. He was a stubby man with a full figure and a salt-and-pepper, matted beard that went down to his chest. He had an interesting odour when he walked past. Vivienne couldn't pin exactly what the aroma was, but it was indistinguishable from the smell of an old antique store. Monsieur Belan approached the board and wrote in capital letters the word 'history'.

'In a few words or less, tell me what this word means to you. Now, I don't know your names yet, so just be patient. You, the gentlemen at the back.' He pointed.

'Well,' the boy stalled. 'I associate history with my ancestors and their culture, I suppose.' Vivienne did not yet know who this boy was, but she would soon enough.

'I like that approach. What's your name, sir?'

'Adrion,' he responded.

'Well, Adrion, for our first introductory topic, we'll be researching our family name and writing a report on what we find.'

Vivienne was not ecstatic about the task. However, she was sure she had a great uncle or someone of the sort that had done something impressive.

After her class concluded, she journeyed back to her apartment, the sun setting in front of her, the sky filled with colours of maroon and magenta. When she arrived, a sudden weak feeling coursed through her body, and she quickly reached for the wall. She opened the fridge—inside, it contained a punnet of raspberries from the day before and two individual yoghurt tubs.

'A meal fit for a king.' She chuckled to herself.

The week had flashed by quickly. Vivienne visited Professor Clarke's office and handed in the essay that was assigned to the class, keeping a low profile. A sudden sadness surged over her as she walked out the university gates, realising she'd not had a meaningful interaction for days besides a couple of conversations with her mother over the telephone. Charging through her apartment, she paced to the balcony door and flung it open. The night was mild, and the air carried relief. Vivienne had four layers of clothing on. It was not the weather that was causing her to chill this particular evening—instead, it was the lingering loneliness that she faced. She poured a glass of whisky and let her sadness slowly dissolve.

CHAPTER THREE

The room was tense, all eyes on Vivienne and Amelie. 'The moral of the novel is that doing what is legally just is not always what is necessarily fair,' Vivienne argued. 'Although Léo gets caught and sentenced for the murder of the baker, we must consider that his actions were only carried out to sustain himself and his daughter. The bigger evil in this story is the society that has failed their duty of care to the people who are suffering out of poverty,' she exclaimed, almost out of breath.

'Yes, although regardless of there being a systemic issue within their society, you cannot deny that Léo's actions were wrong. Léo caused not only his own pain and suffering but had an adverse effect on several of those around him, including the murder of the baker. What about his innocence and right to life?' Amelie said. 'Him being imprisoned for murder was just and therefore fair.' Her words lingered throughout the room.

'Bravo, girls,' Professor Clarke said, slowly clapping. 'Both points were beautifully articulated.' The girls looked at each other and sat back in their seats. 'Our next class discussion will be on this text.' She walked around the room handing out bound pamphlets to each student, containing no more than eight or nine pages. 'We will pick a theme to explore next term once you have read the passage,' she announced and dismissed the class. Vivienne neatly stacked her books and slid them into her bag before exiting the classroom.

'Vivienne,' a voice shouted from behind.

'Amelie.' She responded with uncertainty. Amelie stopped, then stretched closer to her until there was less than a meter between them. 'I just wanted to say that I really enjoyed your outlook on today's discussion.'

'Thank you. you were great as well.'

'I know I get passionate about the topics, but it's all in good spirit, right?' It felt as if Amelie was trying to apologise, which Vivienne instantly hated, because that meant Amelie thought her debating skills were inferior. Vivienne allowed the comment to swoop over her head and nodded, as Amelie clearly had more to say. 'On another note, though, I was wondering if maybe you would like to come back to mine for a drink?'

Vivienne stuttered. 'Oh, I—'

'Come on, it'll be fun,' she interrupted reassuringly. Besides extended family in Paris, Vivienne didn't know many other people. Amelie was intelligent, exuberant, and surprisingly amicable. She had a sense of divinity about her, with her rich brown skin and piercing, dark-green eyes.

'You know what? Yes. Why not?' Vivienne agreed, now surrendering to the invite. 'But first, I have to go home and freshen up.'

'All good.' Amelie laughed while pulling out a small notepad and pen from her bag—the type of notepad where the pen had a personal holder made of felt. Vivienne appreciated Amelie's organisational skills, instead of having to wait and watch as she rummaged through her bag. 'Here's my address. I'll see you around seven?'

'Yes, definitely.'

'Sounds like a date,' Amelie said, then turned around and walked the opposite direction.

Vivienne was amazed by the encounter. She wasn't sure what sparked it. Almost three months they had been in the same class together and not one interaction occurred between them. Until now.

Vivienne stepped into the shower and turned the handle next to the faucet as far left as possible. She liked her showers hot, to the point where most people would blister. However, she had built up a thick tolerance over the years. Extremities were something she often dabbled in—some more dangerous than others. Once out of the shower, she pulled the loose note from her bag containing the address. Coincidentally, she already knew where the street was. One of her aunts lived only two blocks down. In Vivienne's closet were several pieces of niche clothing, ranging from velvet blazers to cashmere turtlenecks. Not to mention the absurd amount of designer pants she owned. Vivienne was fifteen when she found her first job, which was at a small deli only a five-minute walk from her house. Small, though, didn't equate to *unbusy*. Vivienne was never short of tasks and errands to do. She finally had access to money besides the occasional pocket change she received from her parents. With this came not only responsibility, but desire. She would peer through the windows of expensive stores, slightly fogging the glass, while imagining herself dressed in all the lavish clothing. She decided to be smart with her spending, though. A small portion of her weekly salary would be set aside for saving, which she kept behind one of the shelves in her room. The rest would be gone within a blink of an eye.

Vivienne pulled from the closet a black dress with an embroidered, white floral pattern running up the side. She slipped into a pair of platform high heels and then grabbed the clutch bag that she had used that day. The streets were quiet and dimly lit as she walked towards Amelie's place. She noticed some of the houses had Christmas wreaths hanging from the front doors, which reminded her of the festive spirit that her apartment was in desperate need of. She turned her head from left to right as she approached the street, looking at apartment numbers. 'Twenty-four. Twenty-four,' she murmured to herself. Eventually, the number in front of her matched the discreet muttering. Vivienne looked up to see one of the grandest buildings she had ever borne witness to, with seven marble steps that led to the front door. She noticed that there weren't any apartment numbers, only a singular doorbell. A soft tapping sound resonated from the floor above, as the doorbell chimed through the house.

'Vivienne, come in, come.' Amelie opened the door, exposing the sublime interior.

'Which level is your apartment on?' Vivienne said, peering into the house, confused.

'Apartment?' She responded, even more confused. 'Oh, no, this is my house. Well, technically, it's my parent's house, but I'm living here at the moment.'

'You own all three storeys?'

'Well, yes, of course.' She chuckled. 'It's freezing outside, are you coming in?'

Vivienne walked through the front door, first noticing the spiral staircase that was to the far right of the entrance, which coiled over itself twice, followed by the enormous chandelier directly above her.

'Your place is . . . stunning, Amelie.'

'It's been in the family for a few hundred years. Needs some redecorating, if you ask me.' Vivienne thought the exact opposite—she respected its plush ambiance and lack of symmetry. She liked that some of the furniture was mismatched. Not in a tacky way, but in an antique way. 'I just finished preparing dinner.' Amelie pulled a large, steaming pot from the oven. 'It's nothing special, but I *can* assure you it tastes great.' She grabbed two bowls and ladled the mixture into them. 'Here you go.' Amelie passed one of the bowls to Vivienne and directed her to the lounge room.

There was no awkwardness between them. Vivienne felt that she knew Amelie, or more precisely, she could feel her intention. They had such similar interests and aspirations, it felt as if Vivienne were talking to a—much wealthier—version of herself. They both wanted to pursue writing in one form or another. Amelie mentioned wanting to write about travel, and then mentioned further that it would require her to first actually travel. They also both enjoyed drinking. Amelie loved partying and dressing up. There was also something about her that was dark, a yearning of some sort that Vivienne had noticed. But what could someone who lived in a place so grand yearn for? Vivienne cleaned the rim of her bowl with her tongue and passed it to Amelie, who carried the crockery downstairs and returned with a bottle of champagne. 'Cheers, to new beginnings,' she sang as she poured.

'Cheers, to almost completing our first term.'

'Completing is a strong word. Surviving's more fitting.' They leant against one another, laughing.

'That piano, does it work?' Vivienne asked as the laughter ceased.

'Indeed, it does.'

'Can I?' Vivienne asked, gesturing towards the seat. She put her glass of champagne aside and sat in front of the piano. It had been a while since she had played, however, when she began, it was as though she had never stopped. Her favourite arrangement of pieces were by Erik Satie. They were simplistic but angelic. The room was silent as she played. Her head nodded to the chords, her fingers lingering above the keys. She was truly magnificent.

Vivienne admired the house one last time as she gathered

her things and prepared to leave. 'After Christmas, would you be interested in staying with my family and I at our vineyard? It's about two and a half hours from here,' Amelie suggested, as they made their way to the door.

'How could I say no?' It may have been a touch early within the friendship to go away with Amelie. She barely knew her, but she desperately needed to break the monotony in her life.

'I'll keep you posted. Call me anytime.'

'I will.' Vivienne turned her head and waved her hand behind her as Amelie closed the door.

Vivienne woke to a slight hangover the morning after visiting Amelie. She dragged herself out of bed and directly to the coffee machine, which at that moment in time was her most valued possession. Twisting the portafilter, she watched as the hot stream of coffee poured into the cup. Vivienne picked up her small, portable radio and sat on the kitchen bench, her feet dangling and hitting the cupboard below. According to the broadcast, it was the sixth coldest winter on record in France.

'I could have told you that just by looking out my balcony window, for God's sake,' she teased. A foul mood fluttered through the air, as the inability to open the balcony doors from the build-up of sleet consumed her. It was the last day of university for the term and Christmas was approaching, fast. Her mother placed an uncanny amount of importance on Christmas. Everything had to be down to a tee, from the decorations to the food. And God forbid something happened in the kitchen. One year, Marion, in her frantic haze, overcooked a chicken and almost had a stroke. When her family arrived, though, Marion would make the preparation sound effortless. 'I just made something small' was her usual rehearsed line.

Before she had time to worry about the encroaching Christmas antics, she desperately needed to hand out her resumé. Vivienne knew that the small amount of money she had saved for university was not going to last forever. She made the journey down to the plaza near her house and entered a clothing store, which seemed respectable. The lady at the counter explained that they already had enough staff. Vivienne continued, first handing in her resumé at places she liked, but after every rejection, her pickiness faded. One woman informed her that many had lost their jobs recently and finding work was tough. She managed to hand out three or four resumés, although she had a sneaking suspicion that the owners were only trying to be polite. Vivienne rolled up her sleeve and glanced at her watch and cursed under her breath. The chaos of the morning had distracted her from the fact that she had a lecture to attend. She tucked the papers into her leather satchel and sprinted down the street. The lecture had already begun and the walk to the university was approximately ten minutes, five if she ran. The reason for her urgency wasn't because the lecture was important, but merely the fact that she had been late to over a third of her classes. She had earned quite the reputation amongst the students. Her peers started referring to her as 'Vacant Vivienne'. Vivienne ran through the corridor and snuck into the room. 'Ah, Vivienne, so nice for you to finally join us,' Professor Clarke said in a slightly sarcastic tone. 'Your intelligence doesn't make up for your constant absence. Just reminding you.'

The class stared her down as she wandered to her seat. It wasn't the first time that week this had happened either.

'You amaze me.' Amelie grinned, trying to contain her laughter.

The class felt as if it had passed quickly, which Vivienne was grateful for. She couldn't bear another minute of the professor's harsh eyes beating down on her. As she tried to scurry away, Professor Clarke approached her desk.

'Vivienne,' she sighed. 'What is the excuse for your absence this time?'

'I'm sorry, I was handing out my resumés this morning and I lost track of time.'

'I don't want this continuing. You're a bright girl, just get here on time. Okay?' Professor Clarke's intense stare had mellowed out.

'Yes, of course,' she replied sincerely.

'Did you manage to find anywhere hiring?'

'Unfortunately not.'

Professor Clarke walked to her desk and grabbed a small beige booklet from one of the drawers and returned to where Vivienne was seated. 'I know this gentleman.' The words barely left her tongue while she flicked the pages. 'Here we go,' she said, louder now. 'His name is Hugo. He owns a small publishing firm, and last I heard, he's in search of a new assistant . . . if that is something you're interested in,' she added.

'Very interested.'

'There's likely going to be other people who want the job, so you need to have this interview as soon as possible. I will give you his work address and maybe you can pay him a visit tomorrow in the early afternoon. And make sure you tell him Suzan Clarke sent you.'

'Thank you.' Vivienne smiled, reiterating her gratitude.

'My pleasure. However, punctuality next term, young lady.'

It was the day of the interview and Vivienne couldn't contain her anticipation. Real work within the industry that she was prepared to sell a kidney to be in was priceless. The firm was two storeys, with stone walls and a pale, mint-green door. Vivienne arrived to see a room with four desks lined up to her left, an office towards the back, and a staircase on her right. She presumed that the room at the back was where she'd find Hugo. She knocked on the door gently three times. 'Come in,' Hugo announced. He was about six foot, blond, and quiet. Quiet in an assuring way. Humble would have been the most fitting term to describe him. The interview started with the common formalities of introductions, however, quickly digressed into casual conversation. He clarified the requirements of the job and explained that he was in search of someone reliable and dedicated. Vivienne always showed dedication to anything she committed to. Reliability was a debatable quality of hers. She nodded along to the terms of her employment as if she were preparing herself to dance. 'So how does that sound, Vivienne?' Hugo concluded.

'I mean, the hours are manageable, and I don't really—' A fumbled attempt to talk rolled from her mouth. 'Yes, if you'd have me, I would love to work here,' Vivienne said, composed.

'I look forward to working with you.'

'Likewise, Hugo.'

Relief trickled over her as she arrived back to her apartment. She poured herself a generous glass of Pinot Grigio and, with some pleading and prodding, managed to unlock the balcony doors. This was what contentment felt like.

CHAPTER FOUR

There were nine people seated at the table: Vivienne's parents, Marion and Louis, as well as her three cousins, two aunts, uncle, and herself. Everyone seated was from her mother's side. Louis wasn't fond of his family. He despised them. Vivienne remembered the stories he told her as a child. He never explicitly told her what had happened to him, but he alluded that they were terrible people who had done terrible things. As a child, Vivienne thought they might have been murders or part of the Mafia. She learned later from Marion that it was more sinister than that. They stripped Louis of his innocence, of his childhood. The bruises hurt, but it was the neglect that made him sob most nights. He wanted to be loved above anything. When Louis was eighteen, he turned his back on his parents and moved away to live with relatives close to Montreuil. Not long after, he met Marion. Vivienne always hoped to one day be as irrevocably in love as they were.

'You're going to burn it, I'm telling you.'

'No, I'm not. Just sit down, will you?' Marion yelled from the kitchen. She and her sister were constantly at each other's throats, ever since they were children. The sibling rivalry always got the better of the two. Marion raced back and forth from the kitchen, placing down platter upon platter of food, until an instant feast was created.

'This smells amazing, Marion.'

'Is that lamb?'

'Can you pass the bread, please?'

Incomplete sentences and muffled noises bounced off the walls as everyone scrambled to put their favourite food on their plate. It was organised chaos and the one time a year where Vivienne enjoyed not being able to hear her own thoughts.

After dinner, they gathered in the loungeroom, where an apple strudel and a bowl of whipped cream was passed around. The fireplace crackled as Louis placed another log on top of the embers. Her cousin's legs dangled off the sofa as her uncle settled in, ready to share his most interesting travel stories. They *were* interesting, however, Vivienne knew everyone was listening to get a laugh out of his poor impersonation of an English accent.

Vivienne poked her head through the kitchen door, where her mother was cleaning the dishes from dinner. 'Come sit, Mama.'

'I'll be there in a minute, I just need to clean up.' Marion looked up at Vivienne with a gentle, doe-eyed expression.

'I can stay while you clean,' Vivienne offered. Marion liked a tidy kitchen and wouldn't rest until it was spotless.

'Thank you, Vivi.' Marion paused and continued drying a pan. 'First term done, how exciting,' she said after a few seconds.

'I guess.'

'Come on, I haven't seen you for weeks and all I get is "I guess".'

'I met a new friend—her name's Amelie. I'm going to a vineyard in Tours with her family next week.'

'See, that's what I want to hear,' Marion said, interested

enough that she put down the pan she was cleaning, dried her hands, and faced Vivienne.

'It'll be nice to get away.'

'You'll need to tell me all about it; I haven't been to a vineyard in years. I hear Tours is nice, though.' She walked closer to Vivienne and stroked her hair back behind her ear. 'I love you, Vivi,' she said, embracing her in a hug and burying her head in Vivienne's shoulder. A small wet patch trailed down the collar of Vivienne's dress. She lifted her mother's head slightly, revealing her glassy eyes and pale face.

'Mama, what's wrong?' In a state of concern, she tilted her head.

'Nothing. I love you, that's all.' Her bottom lip quivered as she strained a smile. 'Now, go sit and enjoy Uncle Paul's story.'

Vivienne hugged her mother one last time, then turned around and wandered back to her position on the sofa. She hobbled across the small gap between the couch and coffee table, tripping over her cousins' legs that were comfortably lying in her way. Uncle Paul's story drifted away into the background, her mother's crying causing an unnerving sensation to fester in the back of her mind.

It was dark outside when Vivienne woke. She opened her bedroom window, allowing fresh air into the stuffy room. The fireplace hadn't been properly smothered the previous night, transforming the house into a sauna. She dragged herself to the bookshelf and plucked one of the books quietly, conscious not to disrupt anyone's sleep. Before moving into her apartment, Vivienne had a few unfinished novels that she had been dying to read. These partially completed books—and her parents—acted as an incentive to come back home. She examined the book, which appeared to be almost finished, then placed two pillows along the wall and covered herself with her duvet.

Gradually the sun seeped through her bedroom window, turning the pages transparent. Her mother's face appeared in the small gap of the door, just before she could reach the last chapter.

'Vivienne?' Marion whispered cautiously, making sure she hadn't interrupted her sleep.

'Yes.' She tilted her book down and glared at her mother.

'Don't look at me like that, I was just checking to make sure you were alive.'

'Well, I'm alive.'

'Everyone's ready to open gifts, and your cousins are getting restless waiting, so come down as soon as you're dressed.'

'Can I come down in a couple minutes? I just have a few more pages left.' An exhausted expression filled her face.

'No, you can finish the book once we're done—be a good host.' Marion's patience seemed to dwindle. 'And look alive.' She swung her hand forward as if she were casting a spell.

Vivienne stared blankly as her mother left, then moaned and picked up the clothes that she had worn the night before. There was a large white stain on the sleeve of her jumper. One of her aunts had been tipsy and spilled the bowl of cream, most landing on the couch but unfortunately catching Vivienne in the crossfire. She entered the living room to see her cousins' faces, eager with anticipation. They were much younger than her, with the eldest being thirteen. It was difficult to be in their presence. It exhausted her to be around children in general. Babies were the exception to the rule. She liked how they stared with their big eyes and said nothing. Vivienne considered herself a low-maintenance individual, so it made her cringe, the idea of having to interact with a small, irritable child who had constant needs.

'Vivienne. Vivienne. This one is for you.' Her youngest cousin ran towards her with a parcel wrapped in Christmas-themed paper.

'Thank you,' Vivienne replied, sincerely as possible. She ripped the gift open, and in the centre was an elegant silver wristwatch.

'It's from all of us. We hope you like it,' Uncle Paul said. She was pleasantly surprised when she saw the watch. Last Christmas, she'd received a cheap snow globe with a reindeer inside whose antler fell off after a few shakes, so this present was a step up.

'I love it,' Vivienne said with approval—this time without forced sincerity—and watched as her cousins squabbled over their right to the next present.

Vivienne picked up the small bag that she had brought with her and tossed it into the boot of the car. Her father leant on the front door, waving, as Marion and Vivienne reversed out of the driveway and headed towards her apartment. The moon pressed against the darkening sky and the spots of orange projected onto the clouds disappeared one by one. She rolled down the car window and placed her hand out, allowing the cold to turn her fingers numb.

Marion parked at the front of the apartment and scrambled to retrieve Vivienne's bag.

'Thank you for driving me.'

'No problem. Here, give me your bag, I'll help you upstairs.'

'It's one bag, I should be fine,' Vivienne responded. Marion looked into her eyes, again with a similar melancholy expression to the previous night. 'You know you can tell me if there is something wrong, right?'

'I'm losing my baby girl, that's all.' Her voice trembled. Vivienne didn't know what to say to comfort her mother. Instead, she lifted her up a few inches from the ground and spun around in circles until Marion had no choice but to laugh.

'I'm not going anywhere. You're going to *wish* you could get rid of me,' Vivienne said, trying to catch her breath. 'I'll visit once I'm back from Amelie's. I promise.'

'Okay.' Marion grinned.

She watched as her mother's car faded into the distance, then made her way up the stairs. When she entered, the smell of soil swarmed her nostrils. The row of pot plants on her kitchen counter had been knocked over, with the two pots that grew basil and thyme being shattered on the floor and unsalvageable. She adjusted her gaze to see that the window had been left slightly ajar. When she inspected closer, she noticed a soft licking sound drifting from the kitchen. A tiny black cat emerged from behind one of the cabinets, its tail brushing across the wall. She didn't know what to do with the uninvited four-legged guest, but she knew she was tired, and that it was a problem for the morning.

A muffled knock echoed through the apartment. 'Vivienne, open up,' Amelie said with urgency.

She darted towards the door. 'A little patience would go a long way.'

Amelie was startled as she set foot in the room. 'Your cat gave me a heart attack. Also, since when did you have a cat?'

'Since last night, I suppose.' Vivienne shrugged her shoulders.

'Interesting.' She laughed, as she stared down at the dirt footprints that were infrequently dispersed across the floorboards.

'Sorry about the mess.'

'Trust me, I don't care. What I will care about, though, is if you're not dressed within the next thirty seconds.'

'Alright, I'm going.' Vivienne turned her back and waved her hands jovially. She dressed and stuffed into her suitcase her toothbrush and a few extra clothes. Amelie grabbed Vivienne and impatiently ushered her out the door. When they reached the street, Vivienne froze in complete awe.

'What's wrong?' Amelie asked.

'Nothing,' Vivienne said, trying to act nonchalant as she stared at the burgundy red Bugatti in front of her. It was hard to put Amelie's family's wealth into perspective, and even harder to gloss over the fact that she was staring at a car worth more than her house.

'Here, let me take your bag,' Amelie offered. Vivienne never classified herself as a car enthusiast, but this car had a raw, undeniable sensuality about it.

The journey to Tours was lengthy and Amelie's awful navigational skills hadn't made the drive any faster. Two wrong turn offs caused a three-hour drive to turn into five. Vivienne had found it funny above anything else—there was never a dull moment with Amelie. She had her hair down as the radio played, singing along to every song that came on. Even to songs she didn't know. Vivienne's reservations disappeared when she was with Amelie. She hadn't felt that comfortable in someone's presence since Thomas.

The car slowly came to a halt as they turned into the property. She peered out the window to look at the breath-taking manor. It was massive, but an insignificant dot compared to the land it occupied. The place was filled with fields as far as the eye could see. Rows of dense, pruned shrubs ran across most of the property. It was winter, so nothing was growing, just the remnants of the harvest. That was irrelevant and actually preferable, as it meant there was no chance of running out of wine to drink.

'Vivienne, so nice to meet you,' Amelie's father said loudly, as her parents approached the car. 'I'm Gabriel and this is my wife, Julia.'

Vivienne stepped out and kissed both their cheeks. 'Such a lovely place you have down here.'

'Thank you, we try our best. We definitely need to show you around, but we're conscious that you've had a lengthy drive, so we'll let you rest this afternoon,' Julia said endearingly. 'I trust

Amelie will settle you in, but if you need anything, you will find us pottering around.'

'Sounds great.' Vivienne's eyes drifted back to the manor. How it would have been nice to have more many than to know what to do with.

'Alright, we'll be off.' Amelie turned to her mother and father and hugged them, then whispered something inconspicuously into their ears.

The house was two storeys, with a large central staircase that began wide, then constricted like an hourglass before splitting into two separate stairways leading to different areas of the house. The ceilings were high, and every doorway had a unique architrave. The door to the kitchen had wooden flowers etched into it. Amelie led Vivienne to her room on the second storey, then continued to show her around the rest of the estate. Apart from the house, there were three other, smaller buildings. Towards the back of the house was a tennis court with a small outdoor bungalow attached. Directly behind that was a glass greenhouse overrun with a variety of different plants. A bit unkept but still acceptable. The final building was *la cave à vin*, in all its glory. The cellar had a wraparound veranda, and along it were three dining tables fit for hosting.

The day after they had settled, Amelie's parents took them into Tours. The town had beautiful restaurants and old tutor-styled homes. Every shop owner that they passed seemed to know Gabriel and Julia. Vivienne had only known them for two days, however she could tell that they were important. They were part of the haute bourgeoisie, Amelie had explained briefly. Her father had inherited a legacy that extended back hundreds of years. Her mother also came from a wealthy household. Gabriel was considered old money whereas Julia came from a family of entrepreneurs that migrated to France. She also told Vivienne that her mother had been the epicentre of a serious scandal. Julia's parents where both white, so when she was born dark skinned, the family knew that her mother had had an affair. It caused copious issues in their family that Amelie wasn't eager to go into detail about. Julia never knew who her real father was. The family was satisfied, though, once she had married into affluent blood. Vivienne could tell that Amelie's parents were not in love. She knew what true love looked like—as a child, she was constantly surrounded by it. She understood that marriage didn't always equate to love. They seemed content, although love and contentment were two different things.

'Luca,' Gabriel yelled as he approached one of the restaurants.

'Ah, Gabriel. Long time, no see,' Luca said, kissing him on either cheek. 'How's school going, Amelie? What year are you in now?'

'Graduated,' she corrected him.

'Wow, they grow up so fast, don't they? Here, let me take you to your table.' All four of them followed Luca as he directed them to a back room. They were greeted by a table draped with a white tablecloth and chic silverware. The restaurant was expensive, but Vivienne could tell that this room was exclusive. The menus even appeared to be different. Vivienne saw the portions of the meals arrive and felt underwhelmed, but the flavour alone satisfied her.

The lunch finished just before three o'clock, after trivial talks with Amelie's parents about her dreams and aspirations, which felt overly performative. She felt as if she had something to prove.

An uncontrollable thirst hit Vivienne. She tried to avoid thinking about how dry her mouth felt, but she couldn't. The watch next to her read one-thirty in the morning. She didn't want to disturb anyone's sleep by going down to the kitchen to get a glass of water, but her body was begging. Carefully slipping out of bed, she tiptoed along the hall and descended the stairs. When she approached, she noticed the door to the kitchen was closed. On further inspection, there was a small beam of light seeping through the bottom. She crept closer and could hear the sound of two voices. Vivienne stopped for a split second, then put her ear against the door, revealing Gabriel and Julia's voices. As she tuned in, she realised they were not talking but arguing instead.

'You cannot allow your parents to keep treating me like this,' Julia said with distress. Vivienne knew she should have returned to her room, except she was thirsty, and undeniably intrigued. She pressed her ear firmly to the door in an effort to hear the words more clearly.

'I have tried.'

'Well, not hard enough.' There was a slight crack in Julia's voice. 'I will not be continuously punished for what happened. It affected me far more than they could ever fathom. And you know they only bring it up to upset me.' Vivienne's interest reached new heights. What were they talking about? 'Every time I imagine Claudia's lifeless body on the river, my world falls apart. It's as if I have to relive it.' She whimpered and struggled to release the last few words. 'I was grieving, Gabriel, and your parents never stopped blaming me.'

Vivienne tried to understand what was happening, but it was difficult to follow along.

'I lost a child, for God's sake. I couldn't even mourn. The pressure they put me under to have Amelie—but you can't just replace a child!' There was a reflective silence, then a crescendo of footsteps approached the door. Vivienne quickly ran upstairs, ensuring they didn't have time to catch her. She crawled back into bed and attempted to put the snippets of the conversation together. Amelie never talked about having a sister. Chills went down her spine. She knew there was something off about the Chevalier family, but she didn't realise the extent of the skeletons in their closet. She wondered if Amelie knew about this. It wasn't her place to ask, though. It wasn't even her place to know. She was just at the right place at the right time, a fly on the wall. Vivienne went back to sleep, trying to forget what she had heard. Nothing eventful had happened during the visit, not in comparison to that night. Vivienne's main recollection of the trip was the wine. Too much wine. She enjoyed being with her family for the first week, although she did prefer the serenity of being far away from Paris. Amelie understood the quieter side of her personality and never took it personally. It was a rare quality to find in a person. The thoughts of Amelie's dead sister still troubled Vivienne. She hated to admit it, but she wanted to know more. Were there other family secrets?

'I'll drive,' Vivienne said.

'You don't even own a car. When was the last time you drove?'

'Today,' she said, as she got into the driver's seat. Amelie rolled her eyes and smiled. 'You're just going to have to trust me.' She winked.

'I'll let you drive for the first ten minutes.'

'Deal,' Vivienne said and started the ignition.

By the time they arrived at Vivienne's apartment, the sun had fully set and the only light that shone came from the moon and a flickering streetlight.

'I'll see you next week,' Amelie said through the half-rolled-down window.

'No, I think I've had enough of Amelie Chevalier.'

'As if you could get enough of this.' Amelie swung her hands up and down, showcasing herself. Vivienne smiled and waved her down the street. When Amelie was out of sight, she climbed the stairs to her apartment. As she pulled the keys out of her purse, a door unexpectedly opened behind her and Chloe, her next-door neighbour, stepped out.

'Vivienne, glad you're back. just letting you know that there was quite the ruckus coming from your apartment over the past few days,' Chloe announced, with slight passive aggression.

She quickly opened the door to find her apartment in complete disarray. 'Oh my God, the cat.'

'You have a cat?'

'Not really,' Vivienne said in a haze. 'Thank you, Chloe. Sorry about that.'

'No, don't apologise, just wanted to make sure you weren't being robbed.'

'Trust me, I have nothing of value.' Vivienne closed the door and picked up the cat as it pranced out of the bedroom. She stared into its murky brown eyes. 'You just can't stay away, can you?' Vivienne hesitated for a moment. 'I'm going to name you Bonnie.'

CHAPTER FIVE

Hugo rushed out of the office, his tie loose and shirt untucked.

'Vivienne,' he said, slightly out of breath. He placed a thick manuscript on her desk along with a folder and a few loose pieces of paper. 'I really need you to look after this for me today. I've done the majority, just tidy up the last thirty pages. I'm sorry to dump this on you last minute, I forgot I had a meeting with Emma to finalise a few things before first print,' Hugo explained as he tucked the bulk of his shirt in. 'I also have to swing past Marcus's office and persuade him to run the review. Would it kill him not to be an absolute prick?' he said, now talking to himself. The information hurtling towards Vivienne was overwhelming.

'Don't worry, I'll cover everything,' she reassured him.

'I don't pay you enough,' he joked nervously. 'One more thing. Make sure Pierre calls the wholesaler about the distribution issue.'

'I'll keep an eye on it.' Hugo glanced up at Vivienne then down at his watch and proceeded to pace out the building. She saw him through the window drop his leather briefcases as he tried to open the car door without unlocking it.

Vivienne had worked under Hugo's mentorship for over two months and had observed him closely during that time. He was resourceful and talented, yet less methodical than she anticipated. He had let her know that they had been struggling the past few years keeping the company afloat. Larger and more well-renowned publishers started to enter the scene. With better marketing strategies and simply more money, it was hard to find anything worth publishing. Although no longer in his prime, a few lucky breaks managed to keep his business, and pride, intact. He was stressed. On edge constantly. Always forgetting things and always in a constant state of fight. They would sit in his office sometimes and eat lunch together, and this is where she learned that he wasn't as quiet as he seemed. He loved talking about his family and his past success. He never explicitly talked about *his* success but the success of the authors he helped and what they went on to achieve. Vivienne admired his modesty but wouldn't have minded if he took credit for his work every so often. He also liked how tangible his work was. He wasn't just crunching numbers aimlessly at a desk; he was bringing stories to life. It was becoming obvious that Vivienne was an asset to his team, already having helped edit a novel in its entirety. Her job consisted mainly of organising his meetings, running errands, and watching how he worked. Hugo quickly noticed that she was competent and started entrusting her with more significant tasks.

She read through the manuscript that Hugo had put on her desk, leaving notes to the author down the column. It was half past seven in the evening and Hugo hadn't returned. Vivienne tidied her desk and left a sticky note on the thick script with the word 'finished' in capital letters.

Monsieur Belan was interesting. Not in a bad way, but certainly not in a good one either. Vivienne never managed to warm up to him. She couldn't pinpoint whether it was his odour or his constant lifeless expression, but definitely one of the two. Some lectures were so unstimulating that she would sit quietly and imagine all the ways she would get away with murder. This was one of her favourite past times, which involved creating scenarios and figuring out all the ways she could somehow escape. Some of these scenarios became so intricate that she would have to revisit them later. Vivienne was, however, finding this lesson particularly interesting. It wasn't Monsieur Belan's lecture that had caught her attention, although his rant about political corruption was surprisingly fascinating—it was something else. Vivienne had never found someone she was genuinely attracted to, though then again, she had never really stopped and looked. She fell in love with some men. Unfortunately, all of them were encased between the pages of bound books. But when Vivienne looked at Adrion, she felt something strange. She was unable to take her eyes off him. He wasn't obnoxious or trying to impress anyone. He had dark, wavy hair which covered the upper part of his forehead and was shorter at the back. She loved his hands and the way he gripped his pen. Vivienne loved the unknown. She wanted to explore someone in depth. Read them like a book and understand their intent. It took a lot to spark her interest, but once her attention was attained, it was impossible to shake. Only recently had she been having these strong feelings for him, but she had never acted on them. In her mind, acting on these feelings was not a viable option. Though unrealistic, she was hoping that he would approach her after class confessing that she was on his mind. Vivienne had to remind herself that her life wasn't a poorly scripted romance novel. She decided that a move had to be made and soon. After class had ended, she contemplated talking to him but was quickly discouraged by the fear of embarrassing herself.

'Vivienne.' Amelie appeared next to her as she walked down the corridor.

'I didn't know you had a class today,' Vivienne said, slightly startled.

'I don't, I just had to hand something into Professor Clarke. Nothing important.'

She turned her head towards Amelie. 'We're still on for tonight, right?'

'How about you just come over now? I could definitely use your culinary skills,' Amelie joked.

'You could *definitely* use a world-renowned chef. My services are costly, though, do you think you can manage?'

'Don't worry, I can manage.' She nudged Vivienne and smiled.

Amelie and Vivienne arrived at the house, which had just been freshly cleaned by the family's maid. Vivienne had become quite familiar with Amelie's residence, spending almost every second day there. It didn't make sense to stay crammed in her own apartment. She even had her own drawer in Amelie's room where she kept some of the clothes that wouldn't fit into her own wardrobe.

'I think we need to discuss your fridge situation.'

'Why, what's wrong with it?' she said, shuffling past Vivienne.

'You have three carrots, a singular piece of mozzarella, and mustard.' Vivienne reached further into the fridge as if food would magically appear.

'I don't see a problem.' Amelie opened her kitchen cupboard and looked inside. 'I also have a zucchini that looks like it needs to be used soon. And eggplants. Oh, and pasta that only expired a month ago.' Vivienne brought all the ingredients out of the fridge and placed them on the island counter.

'I reckon we can make this work. But tomorrow, you and I are going to the market,' she added while sniffing the mustard and trying to conjure a recipe idea.

Vivienne began to dice up the vegetables and sauté them,

then boiled the water in preparation for the pasta. As she cooked, Amelie told her theories of what she thought had happened to her dog that went missing when she was a child. The theories ranged from abduction to cult sacrifice, and Vivienne was living for it. Amelie could somehow make the most interesting conversations out of thin air. Vivienne took two plates from the glass cabinet and served up the improvised dish. Amelie kept talking, until her mouth exhausted every other topic, and her love life was all that was left. Furthermore, the lack thereof. There was one boy who was interested in her, but similarly to Vivienne, she had extremely high standards when it came to romance.

'We need to find you someone,' Amelie mentioned out of the blue after a pause in her rambling. 'Do you have your eye on anyone at the moment?' she looked at her intensely, searching her soul.

'No, not really,' Vivienne said, in a smitten tone.

'No way, there is someone, isn't there? Go on, do tell.'

'Fine. Someone I take history lectures with. We've only talked a few times. Actually, once, and he asked if I had a pen. But there is something about him,' she admitted, while running her fingers across the rim of her glass.

'Is he attractive?' Amelie asked.

'Very attractive. But it's more than that.'

'Name?'

'Adrion Ferro.'

'You have to make a move.' Amelie appeared utterly invested in Vivienne's new love interest, her face stuck in intense thought before standing with a newfound purpose. 'You know what you need to do. Call him,' she proposed with excitement.

'Are you serious—'

Before she could finish her sentence, Amelie had returned with the phone directory that she kept underneath her bed.

'Trust me, when it comes to men, sometimes you need to have an assertive approach.' This theory seemed somewhat farfetched, however, she had never been in relationship before. Maybe Amelie was right to some degree.

'Fine—Yes, I'll do it.'

'Wait, really?' Amelie was surprised as she slid the book across the floor. Vivienne opened it and flicked through until she came across his name. There were two Adrion Ferros. She ruled out one, as he lived too far away to be *her* Adrion, and was left with one telephone number staring back at her. Amelie stretched the cord of the rotary until it reached Vivienne's hand. She shook a little as she dialled the numbers. Was she really doing this? The phone was picked up within seconds, although it felt as if it had been hours.

'Hello, who's this?'

Her heart rate spiked. 'It's Vivienne.' She hesitated. 'Vivienne LaRue.'

'Oh, Vivienne. From Monsieur Belan's class, right?' She froze and looked at Amelie, who was next to her eavesdropping on the conversation.

Amelie prodded Vivienne with her elbow. 'Continue,' she whispered as quietly as she could, which in retrospect was as far from quiet as possible.

'Yes, that's me,' she went on.

'What's up?'

'Nothing much.' Amelie inaudibly gasped and rolled her eyes at Vivienne out of frustration.

'Why are you calling me, exactly?' Adrion asked.

She was uncertain what to do next. Before she had time to articulate a proper sentence, the words started flooding from her mouth.

'I've been watching you, Adrion, and I think we should go out sometime.' Vivienne stumbled over her words and tilted the phone away from herself, attempting to regain confidence.

'As in a date?'

'Yes, as in a date.' There was a minor halt. Vivienne's heart pulsated against the walls of her chest, her ribs sore from the pounding.

'Okay. I have a lecture tomorrow afternoon, but how about dinner?'

'Sounds good,' Vivienne said, surely.

'What's your address? I'll pick you up around seven.'

'28 Rue Rene.'

'Perfect, I'll see you then.'

Before Vivienne could say anything else, static started bouncing from the telephone. She expected Adrion to be perplexed by her call, yet he seemed calm and unfazed, almost though he had been expecting her, as ridiculous as it may have sounded. Amelie sat across from Vivienne with her hand over her mouth and eyes wide. She didn't have to say a word—the shock on her face summed up how both of them were feeling.

Amelie brewed a cup of tea and laid down on the sofa. Vivienne appeared from the bedroom in a plain red dress.

'I don't like it,' Amelie expressed, glancing up from the magazine she had found lying on the coffee table.

'You didn't like the two before either,' she replied, irritated.

'All I'm saying is that the dresses you've tried on so far have made you look—'

'Like a whore?' Vivienne interrupted her and smirked.

'Poor choice of wording. I was going to say . . . promiscuous. You don't want to reveal too much on the first date. Leave something to the imagination. Do you have something more modest?'

'Yes, but most look like they're out of the eighteenth century.'

'Okay, well, try one of those on.' She returned to her magazine as Vivienne simultaneously hopped to her room and unzipped the dress. This time when she re-emerged from the bedroom, a flowy white dress with puffed sleeves was perfectly tailored to her body.

Amelie put down her magazine and scanned the dress with her eyes. 'You're telling me this was just . . . in your closet?'

'It was my mother's. Do you like it?' Vivienne walked closer to Amelie and turned around slowly until she reached her original position.

'I don't just like it. I love it.'

Vivienne took the dress off, pleased with herself, and placed it on her bed carefully, making sure it didn't crease or catch on anything. Adrion was expected to arrive within the next half hour. Nerves had caught the better of her the entire day. With no classes or work, the preparation for their date had consumed her. She tried preoccupying herself with a long morning walk and Amelie, but her mind kept worrying about the ways she might ruin her chance with Adrion.

'You're going to be fine,' Amelie comforted her. 'Just be yourself, and maybe bring down the intensity just a notch.'

'I've never done this before.'

The faint sound of tyres screeching from outside her apartment came into earshot, closely followed by a car door closing.

'There's no pulling out now.'

'Fuck.'

Vivienne ran to the bathroom one last time, quickly fixing any blemishes. She was never paranoid in her appearance, but this was a special occasion.

'You look gorgeous.'

'Thank you.' Vivienne hugged Amelie, then unlocked the door. 'Lock up once you leave. Or stay the night, whatever works.'

She slowly walked down the stairs, mentally preparing herself. Her mouth felt dry, and her neck slightly shone with sweat. She took one deep breath and exited the building. Adrion leant against his car, the wind gently blowing against his face, making his hair unkept.

The car door extended open, inviting her in.

'Glad you showed up.' She stretched her hand towards him, instantly regretting it. Adrion grabbed it and raised it to his mouth, gently kissing it. She thanked God that he hadn't realised she was reaching for a handshake. There would have been no coming back from that.

'I had all intentions of coming,' he said, holding the door as she stepped in.

'Where are we going tonight?'

Adrion turned to her in the passenger seat. 'Don't worry, you'll see.'

CHAPTER SIX

The candle shone in the centre of the table, casting silhouettes on the walls around them. The restaurant was empty, and the waiters and waitresses stood patiently in the kitchen, with their discreet conversations and occasional glances. Vivienne was unbothered, too engrossed in her own conversation with Adrion. She had been observing him the entire night, every subtle detail. From how often he maintained eye contact to the singular dimple he had when he smiled. He had a beautiful smile that made her forget what she was going to say. Vivienne looked for every possible indication that he wasn't worthy. All she needed was a single red flag that would allow her to pounce like a bull and bail. But she couldn't find one. Her philosophy consisted of one key concept when it came to relationships, whether they were platonic or romantic. 'A knife couldn't hurt you if you didn't step forward'. She was conflicted though. She wanted to feel loved. She wanted to be vulnerable, but she found it difficult to accept the pain that accompanied vulnerability. Their conversation was interrupted as one of the waitresses wandered to their table—irritated—and informed them that they were supposed to close twenty minutes ago. Vivienne lifted her bag, prepared to pay, but before she could rummage through her purse, Adrion had slid the bill towards him.

'No. That's not how this works.' She smiled.

'This is exactly how it works.'

'What? 'Cause you're the man?'

'No, because next time, you're paying. And the place I'm thinking of won't be cheap,' Adrion teased as he slipped the money into the slim black folder and handed it to the waitress.

The evening was fresh. They made their way to the front of the restaurant where Adrion took off his black coat and placed it over Vivienne's shoulders.

'What are you doing?' she asked.

'Thought you might be cold.' She was in fact cold. Wearing his coat, though, would have made her seem like a hopeless romantic. And she wasn't prepared to reveal her sappiness just yet.

'I'm not cold.'

'Well, that's pretty extraordinary, because I'm freezing my arse off.'

'You're right, I am pretty extraordinary.'

'Oh, and modest too.'

'Modesty only looks good on monks.'

Adrion laughed. 'And funny. This list is getting long.' He twisted his head and looked at Vivienne, who had fallen behind a few steps. The car was parked in a pitch-black alley a few hundred metres from the restaurant, and they had almost missed it when roaming down the pavement.

Vivienne peered out the car window as they drove. 'I've always loved it there,' she said, pointing in the direction of the botanical gardens across from the university. Once her lectures had finished, Vivienne would sometimes bring a book and a notepad and sit in an enchanting spot she had found, full of overgrown vines and purple flowers. It was nice to be alone in nature and feel the ground alive beneath her. It reminded her that she was part of something bigger. As far as she knew, the spot she held dear was unknown to the rest of the world.

'I was actually thinking of taking you there on our next date.' He glanced at Vivienne as he turned into her street. 'If you'll have me.'

'Another date will suffice. Was that modest enough?'

'Just because you're dressed like you're from the 1800s doesn't mean you also have to speak like you are too.'

Vivienne hit him playfully and he shrieked, pretending to be fatally wounded. She appreciated his wit. 'It's from the 1930s, for your information, and it's timeless.' Vivienne got out of the car and Adrion rolled down the window. 'Thanks for driving me home. Hopefully I'll have a car soon.' She stared at him amorously.

'All good,' he replied, exchanging a similar look.

Vivienne could feel a rise of sexual tension. 'Would you like to come up and have a drink?' Adrion smiled down into his lap, in an attempt to conceal his grin, then drew his attention back to her. She knew what she wanted. Or at least the blood pumping through her body knew what it wanted.

Adrion hesitated for a moment. 'I better not, it's getting late.'

Patience was a virtue, Vivienne knew that. She wanted to do this right, let the relationship unfold naturally. It was clear that he wasn't motivated by meaningless sex.

'Probably for the best. I think Amelie's sleeping in my room and it wouldn't be wise to get in the way of her and sleep.'

'I'll call you?'

Vivienne nodded. 'I had fun tonight,' she quickly added, as she leant against the entrance of the building with her heels—that had been killing her the entire night—dangling from her hand.

'Me too, Vivienne.'

'Someone had a big night.' Amelie bent over with a steaming mug of coffee. 'Don't leave a single detail out.'

Vivienne made her way into a sitting position in the bed, then grabbed the mug from Amelie. 'At least let me wake up first.'

'Consider this payback for kicking me last night when you got into bed. What time did you get home, exactly?' Vivienne had snuck in during the night, knocking over lamps and bumping into bedside tables. She had stubbed her toe hard getting into bed and the pain had only just resurfaced.

'I think it was around half past eleven,' she said, trying to regain her memory of the previous night.

'So, what was he like? Everything you imagined?'

'And more.' Vivienne sipped on the piping hot coffee. Amelie asked question after question, Vivienne often avoiding a real answer. That night felt so intimate. So private. It may have been selfish, but she didn't feel like sharing it with anyone else. Following a solid half-hour interrogation, Amelie knew she wasn't going to get any more information out of her.

'When are you going to see him again?'

'He said he'll call me later this week. He already has our next date planned out.'

Amelie sighed. 'I'm jealous.'

'Don't worry, we're going to find you someone soon. Plenty of young, eligible bachelors out there.'

'Bold of you to assume that I don't *already* have a man in my life,' she said while stretching her arms to the ceiling and yawning.

'Please, you wouldn't be able to stay quiet about it for more than ten seconds.'

'True.' Amelie nodded her head and made a wide-eyed expression. Vivienne uncovered herself and walked through the apartment. The place was dull, and cold like a morgue. Her high from the previous night was conflicting with the stillness.

'Should we go to the library today? I have to finish the essay we got last week or Professor Clarke is going to have my head on a platter.'

'Crap, that's due soon, thanks for the reminder,' Amelie replied, shaking her head. 'I'll pack my stuff.'

The university library was arguably the best place in all of Paris. Vivienne had managed to make nice with some of the librarians that worked there. Once their loyalty had been won, she had free rein of books and texts that were restricted to the rest of the students—and even some of the faculty. This exclusive selection ranged from first-edition copies of famous novels to even personal diaries and letters from famous authors such as Émile Zola. She didn't know these people personally, but when she read what they had written, it was as if she was there with them. This access made her feel important, as if she was now part of the legacy they had left. She hoped to one day be like that. Have people cherish her work. Be immortal.

A small part of her thought it was cruel to keep these books from people. If it wasn't for her, the books would've faded and rotted away into a distant memory. Maybe she was just being cynical. She wasn't the only person in the world who loved reading, but she believed that growing up in a bookstore made her more refined. The library also provided her with a space to surround herself with people who interested her. She enjoyed random encounters. Sometimes she would sit quietly and read, curled up in her chair, and the next moment, someone would come up and ask her about the book she was reading. And sometimes it would end in an argument. She used to think libraries were a place of quiet and worship, like a church, but her time at the library was—more often than not—the most social part of her day. When an argument did break out, she always had to be right. This was the one area in her life in which she refused to be wrong.

One of the librarians approached them and handed a thick,

forest-green book to Vivienne. 'I managed to bump you up the reserves list,' she whispered, as she passed her the book.

'I've been trying to get my hands on this for weeks.'

'Due date is in two weeks, so you'll have plenty of time.' The librarian winked at Vivienne and marched off, pushing a small trolley of books in front of her.

'Look at you, getting all the exclusives. I need to start playing my cards right.'

'What can I say, they love me.'

Three days had passed and no call from Adrion. Had he been ignoring her? Or worse, he'd forgotten her. Vivienne sat at her desk anxiously, slouched over a paper Hugo had assigned her. Between juggling university and her job at the company, she had slowly been engulfed by a silent pressure that refused to surrender. She felt like she was the pig in the straw house. One small huff would have been enough for things to start crumbling.

The phone suddenly rang. She ignored the first three rings, too immersed in her work, then swiftly stood up at the fourth ring, realising the possibility of Adrion at the end of the line. 'Hello. Vivi?' Marion's voice rushed out.

'Oh, hi, Mama.'

'Well, don't be too thrilled by my call.'

'No, I'm happy to hear your voice,' she corrected her. 'I was just expecting someone else.'

'Who were you expecting? A boy?'

'Yes, actually, I was.'

'A shocking turn of events. Who's this gentleman then?'

'His name is Adrion, he's in my history class at the university.'

'He must be pretty amazing to have caught your attention.'

Marion was right. Vivienne smiled to herself. 'Yes. Yes, he is.'

'I want to hear more, but I want to see you in person. You haven't visited in weeks.'

'I know, I've been swamped with work and study,' she said apologetically. She felt guilty being away from her mother. Eighteen years they had spent together, barely leaving each other's side, and now she didn't even see her once a week. A second wave of guilt swarmed her. 'I'll come down this weekend, how does that sound?'

'That sounds great. I'll cook us something nice. Your father will enjoy spending some time with you as well.'

An infrequent tapping sound started travelling from the window near Vivienne's desk. She dismissed it, but after several faint taps, she decided to investigate.

'I have to go, Mama, but I'll see you this weekend.'

'I love you, darling.'

Vivienne hung up the phone in one rapid motion and looked carefully at the window. A pebble bounced off the frame, followed by another. She opened the balcony doors and walked into the gentle night, then looked down, her eyes locking with Adrion's.

'Vivienne.'

'What are you doing here?' She smiled down at him, leaning on the iron rails of her balcony.

'Get dressed. I'm taking you out.' Vivienne changed out of her night gown and slipped into a pair of pants and a lacey camisole, then grabbed her leather jacket. She still needed to finish the papers for Hugo, but they could wait.

'I thought you had forgotten about me.' Vivienne focused her attention on him. Adrion was wearing a pair of Levi jeans and a royal-blue button up. Casual compared to what he wore on their first date.

'I was going to call but I wanted to see you in person.'

'You caught me just in time. I was getting ready for another date. I'll have to postpone now.'

'Is that so?' Adrion smirked as Vivienne moved away from the entrance of her apartment and towards him.

'We better be on our way then.'

'Sure thing, Madam.'

They walked and she observed him, like she had on their first date. He used an absurd amount of hand gestures when explaining something he was passionate about. Anything, for a matter of fact. He was smooth and effortless, and so confident it made her question herself. And when she spoke, he looked at her. Really looked at her.

'it's closed at night. You know that, right?' Vivienne said as they reached the gates.

'I do indeed. Here, follow me.' He walked to his left and started to scout around the perimeter. 'Help me move this.' There was a large, three-foot stump of wood hidden behind one of the trees. They walked behind it, both bending and pushing with as much strength as they had until it hit the wall.

'Breaking and entering. Nice.' Vivienne pressed her hands against her knees, out of breath.

'We don't have to go if you don't feel comfortable.'

'You're too sweet,' she said sarcastically. 'So do you want to go first or should I?' She didn't mind bending the rules. It was public property so technically it wasn't illegal.

'You go first, I'll give you a leg up.' She stepped onto the log and hauled herself over the brick wall. Adrion followed a few seconds behind. 'I know the perfect spot.'

'So do I.'

He paused for a second. 'Lead the way then.'

The garden was filled with ten-storey-high trees that cast dark shadows underneath the moonlight. Flowers sprung from every corner, and the grass smelt crisp, freshly mowed. Vivienne turned sharply to her right and led Adrion through a small gap between some dense bushes. He cut in front of her and started to take the lead. He seemed to be familiar with the route. After two more turns and another set of bushes, they had arrived.

'How did you know where to go?' Vivienne stood there, dumbfounded.

'Well, this is my spot.'

The place was far from the beaten track and almost impossible to find. She genuinely thought she was the only person who knew about it. In all the time she had been coming, how had she not run into him? Adrion approached the small, unmaintained workbench and pulled out a large blanket from behind. He shook it and laid it down on the grass, then pulled a lighter out of his pocket and lit the candle that was wrapped in the blanket.

'Come, sit.' Vivienne laid down next to him, looking up towards the sky. 'I love when the sky's clear like this. Kind of makes you realise how small we are,' he said, loudly exhaling. There was a moment of silence before Adrion grabbed her hand and dragged it upwards.

He closed one eye and guided her finger in a curved motion. 'That's Aries.' Vivienne knew close to nothing about constellations, but she knew Aries was symbolic of the Ram.

'Is Aries the Ram?'

'Yes.'

'Rams typically symbolise strength and power.'

'Would you say you're like a ram?'

Vivienne smiled and looked back at the sky. Adrion stared at her and reached over, moving her dark brown hair away from her eyes and tucking it behind her ear. 'You're so beautiful.'

'And what else?'

He lowered his gaze and looked at her perfect, cupid-bowed lips, then leaned in, his fingers travelling from her forehead to her cheek. She turned to her side and put her hand on his chest, no longer feeling nervous.

'You smell sweet, like jasmine.' He leaned in further. His breath left a warm trail on her skin. Vivienne's lips grazed his, waiting for a response. Adrion stalled for a moment before his mouth pushed back. His hand travelled down her waist, the other intertwined with her hair. He pulled away and looked at her. 'Beautiful is lazy, you're right,' he whispered. His face was still close enough that she could feel his words against her lips. 'You're strong. And irresistible.'

She had been more vulnerable the past week than at any point in her life. Overanalysing things was her worst habit, but in that moment, there was nothing to analyse. He was a person who saw her. Who wanted her.

'Hey, can I borrow the car for the weekend?' Vivienne said, barging through Amelie's front door.

'Sure. What for?'

'I'm going to see Marion for a couple of days.'

'Any news from Adrion?'

'Yes, actually. You won't believe what happened last night. He came to my apartment and started throwing little pebbles at my window to get my attention.'

'How romantic,' Amelie said, entranced, while fiddling with the car keys.

'That's not even the best part. I got dressed and he took me on a date to the botanical gardens.'

'The one next to the university? Isn't it closed past eight?'

'We jumped the fence.'

'You are so bad.' She covered her mouth and laughed.

'We then went to this lovely spot, secluded from the rest

of the place.' Vivienne grabbed Amelie by the shoulders. 'And then he kissed me.'

Amelie reciprocated and grabbed her shoulders. 'I am so fucking proud of you. Someone who throws stones at your windows is definitely a keeper. Men need to start taking pages out of the *Book of Adrion.*'

Vivienne came across cold and reserved, and she knew that people found her unapproachable. They had directly told her before. This wasn't terrible, though; it protected her from unwanted attention. Only the people who truly sought to know her approached her, and it felt like armour. Vivienne was a babushka doll with many complex layers, and although she was driven, she didn't know what she was heading to. But Adrion made sense, and he took away the need to know what the future held.

'Thanks for putting up with me constantly borrowing the car. You're a life saver,' Vivienne said as she grabbed the keys.

'No worries, I'll see you when you're back. Say hello to Marion for me.'

'Will do.' She unlocked the car and jumped in. Vivienne was in desperate need of a car, but she knew when she finally had one, there would be no excuse to take Amelie's. Besides, she was barely financially stable; buying a car would have left her homeless.

Rain started to pour down as she turned into her parents' driveway. She ran inside and made her descent through the hallway, drenched and dripping on the floorboards. The smell of home was comforting, especially after being away for weeks on end.

She took her coat off and laid it on the table. 'Mama?' she called from the dining room. 'Oh, there you are.' Marion faced away from Vivienne as she brewed a cup of tea in a small saucepan.

'Hi, Vivi,' she replied, with her back still turned to her. A small green scarf was wrapped around her head and tied off at the back.

'I didn't realise you were into head scarfs?'

'I'm not.' Marion finally turned around. 'Vivienne.' She hesitated. 'I have cancer.' Marion's voice cracked and she swallowed, almost choking on her words. She pulled the head scarf off, revealing her hairless head. The sentence pierced through Vivienne's body. She looked at her mother and felt like she had been stabbed. With every glance at her head and pale skin, the knife went deeper, twisting, until there was a hole in her chest. The tears were salty on the corners of her lips as she clutched her mother tightly.

Vivienne released her and looked at her, clearing her face of one last tear.

'You're a fighter.' The word cancer conjured in her mind. 'I can't lose you.'

CHAPTER SEVEN

The wait was always lengthy. Vivienne sat in one of the chairs opposite Marion, facing away from the other patients in the room. When she looked at them, all she saw were endless copies of her mother. The room was crammed with mission brown floors, cupboards, and a mission brown reception desk. This colourless place was where people came to die, not survive. In essence, that's what a hospital was: a place where people died. No matter how many lives were saved, or how many bandages had been wrapped and wounds stitched closed, death was the only guarantee life held. It was inevitable.

Dr Dupont appeared from the corridor, in his usual attire—a white shirt and grey suit. He was on the shorter side, with a large belly and round silver glasses.

'Marion Larue.' Vivienne and her mother followed him into his office. 'Please, take a seat,' Dr Dupont said as he opened a folder containing Marion's medical records. 'It's fairly good news from our end. The cancer in your breast has shrunk half the size, and you seem to be coping with the chemotherapy,' he explained without looking up from the folder. 'Now, that doesn't mean you're out of the woods yet. I would still like to monitor you carefully, so fortnightly appointments will continue. There is no need for changes to our current chemo regime.' He continued flicking through the pages of the folder which contained valuable information to him, but absolute jargon to someone like Vivienne. As long as he helped cure her mother's cancer, she didn't care about the means necessary.

'Have you had any reactions to the antiemetics you were prescribed?'

Marion glanced at Vivienne for reassurance, both shrugging with uncertainty. 'Are those the ones to stop the vomiting?'

'Yes.'

'No, they seem to be working fine.'

'Wonderful. I will write you another prescription just in case you run low before I see you again.' He aggressively signed and tore a page from the small book on the side of his table. 'If you stay on this trajectory, the road of remission may not be as long as it seems.'

'Thank you, doctor.'

'I look forward to more good news in the future, Marion.'

Relief latched onto Vivienne's body as they left the hospital. The distinct smell of damp towels and shattered hope was over-whelming. Except she wasn't there to stimulate her senses. She was there to support her mother. The doctors and the nurses at the hospital preached the importance of a 'solid support system'. They explained that illnesses, especially cancer, were not only a physical fight but a mental one too. Vivienne under-stood. She couldn't have imagined going through what her mother had to face. Nor could she bear the thought of one day living life, and the next spending more time in a hospital than her own bedroom. Vivienne had devoted more time to her mother after she was aware of the diagnoses. She was ashamed to admit it, but the cancer had brought them closer in some sense. Her father found it hard to cope some days. Marion reminded him that her illness didn't define her. Underneath the surgical scars on her chest and her pale skin, she was still the woman he married. A woman who sang from the top of her lungs when no was watching. A woman with the capacity to love. A woman with grit and determination. Vivienne sometimes wondered whether she stumped her mother's journey as a person. She couldn't help but feel—more than ever—as if she were a liability. Especially now, with this disease that was so degrading and so consuming. Marion used to tell her as a child that 'if you don't eat life, life will eat you'. Her visits to the hospital made this idea tangible.

Marion lived for Vivienne. Not being a mother would have killed her. Yet Vivienne couldn't help the guilt that flooded her occasionally. The guilt of taking invaluable years away from her mother's life.

'Are you staying for dinner tonight, Vivi?'

'I promised Adrion I would spend the night with him. Sorry.'

'When are you going to introduce me?' she asked, as they both unpacked the groceries they had collected on the way from the hospital.

'When the time is right.'

'And when will that be?'

'We've only been seeing each other for a couple of months. I haven't even met his mother yet.'

'Alright, that's fine.' Marion started unpacking the fruit into a bowl. 'You don't have to give me such cryptic responses. Just say what's on your mind.'

'Fine. Over the summer, once I have more time.' Vivienne looked down at her watch. The one she had received for Christmas. 'Shit, I said I would meet him at six o'clock.'

'Don't worry, the traffic should be light. He'll wait, I'm sure.'

'You're right. Love you—call you tomorrow.' She kissed her mother. 'And you *will* meet him, I promise.'

Vivienne raced out the door towards her small black Volkswagen, her keys in hand. Hugo had become fed up with her constantly borrowing his car to run errands. With some—not-so-subtle—hints from her end, he believed it was more beneficial to buy her something low budget than to continue their constant dilemma. It was considered a company car, but Vivienne was the only one who used it. She was practically the owner.

'Fuck. Sorry I'm late.'

'All good,' Adrion said as he leaned in and kissed her. Vivienne took his hand and strung him along behind her, flicking her head backwards and smiling. She unlocked the apartment and roamed over to the kitchen pantry, pulling out a small square can of tuna.

'Bonnie.' The black cat emerged from the bedroom and jumped in front of her. 'Good girl.' Bonnie purred, as Vivienne scratched the nape of her neck. 'Do you want anything to eat?' she said, while jiggling the tuna out of the can.

'What do you have?' Adrion flipped through the collection of vinyls next to the record player.

'Tuna.'

'Not really in the mood for cat food.'

'I could make tomato soup. They're going bad otherwise. Thoughts?'

'Anything is a step up from a can of tuna. Do you have bread?'

'It's a bit stale, but you'll live.' She reached for the large bunch of red ripe tomatoes, picking off the two that were bruised and had started to grow mold.

'This is some next-level ill treatment, Vivienne. I can assure you hostages get better.' The needle skipped as Adrion placed it over the record. He slowly danced towards her, the smooth saxophone warming the walls.

'Oh, very sexy.'

He grabbed her waist from behind and kissed her gently on the neck. 'How was your mother?' The topic of Marion's cancer was yet to be discussed. There was no reason to. The minute she did, she knew it would become even more of a reality. Besides, the thought of people pitying her left a bitter taste in her mouth. Especially if those people were Adrion and Amelie.

'She's good. But I'd rather not talk about my mother while slow dancing with you.'

'Well, since we're already on the topic of mums, how would you like to meet mine? Tomorrow night?' Vivienne considered the idea. His mother, and her approval, meant a great deal to him, and she didn't want to disappoint.

'That would be nice.'

'I'll let her know. She's been dying to meet you. She'll start cooking the minute I tell her.'

'Sounds like Marion.'

Adrion turned her around by her waist and kissed her lips. 'I want to meet your parents as well soon. Maybe over the break?'

'I'll make sure they find an opening in their busy schedules.'

She no longer had a foot on the ground. She was swept off her feet, gracefully falling. How could this be so perfect? How could he be so perfect?

Vivienne stared blankly at her notes. She had a black strapless dress that could've been nice for the evening. Or was that too provocative? What if Adrion's mother was more conservative? What if Vivienne walked in and there were pictures of Jesus everywhere and she was showing too much cleavage? That would have definitely secured her chance at eternal damnation. Maybe something more casual would've been fitting. Pants with a nice top. Or a floral dress. She had to make a good impression. Sofia's opinion mattered.

The class was coming to an end, and she hadn't listened to a word of the lecture.

'As you all know, we're approaching yet another term's end, and I would just like to say that I have been impressed with the standard of work that you have continuously produced. You should *all* be proud. Enjoy the rest of your day; you've earned it.' Professor Clarke packed her leather bag as the students raced out of the classroom like a stampede. 'Vivienne, could you stay behind quickly?'

She walked to the professor's desk. 'Yes?'

'I found your most recent essay quite intriguing. It was a little dark and definitely not for the faint hearted, but your ideas are truly magnificent. You write so fluently.'

'Thank you, professor.'

'Are you doing any writing besides for your subjects at the university?' she asked, now sat back in her chair with her hands clasped together on the table, waiting for a response.

'I'm working as assistant editor now for Hugo, but it's more editing rather than writing. So I guess not.'

'Do you aspire to write in the future?' Vivienne stopped for a moment and thought. Of course she aspired to write in the future.

'My biggest aspiration is to publish my writing one day. That is, if I have the time to write.'

'I think it's important to make time. If you have an idea, sometimes the best thing to do is put pen to paper. You are quite exceptional, and you always have my full support.' Vivienne at that moment was inspired. An empowered woman and well-regarded author believed in her. It felt like a warm light, guiding her.

'I'll let you know if I decide to write anything.'

'Always. I will see you next week. Take care.'

Vivienne exited the classroom and turned into the corridor. Amelie suddenly appeared from thin air. 'You scared me,' Vivienne said, startled.

'What did Professor Clarke want?'

'Just something about my essay.'

'I can't stay and chat, just wanted to know if you were coming to dinner tonight. Mum and Dad are over,' she said quickly.

'I wish I could but I'm meeting Adrion's mother tonight.'

'Wow, that's big.' Amelie nodded her head. 'How about tomorrow night then? They're in town for a couple of days.'

'Yes, perfect.'

'Good. So sorry I can't talk, I'll see you tomorrow and you can update me then,' she shouted, midway down the corridor. Vivienne was unsure why Amelie had been in such a rush. Nothing made Amelie rush, so it must have been important.

He had been running late, which was strange. Vivienne was usually the unpunctual one in their relationship. Though his absence hadn't fazed her. She was enjoying the last glimpse of sun as it slowly disappeared behind the buildings in front of her. The days had started to become longer, and summer was finally approaching. Her favourite season had always been winter. It was a time where she could burrow herself away from the rest of the world. An excuse not to leave the safety of her home. Summer did have its own special chamber within her heart. She loved the feel of orange juice dripping down her hands as she devoured the flesh. The feeling of the crisp heat and lying in the shade with nothing more than a pair of shorts and a singlet.

'Hello?' Adrion called from below. He had been standing there for a few minutes expecting her to notice. However, the sun had hypnotised her, and almost blinded her too.

'You're a bit late.' She covered her eyes and squinted down at him.

'I know. I fell asleep.' He laughed.

'I guess I can forgive you this one time.'

'And in return, I'll forgive you for the dozen times you've been late.' Vivienne smirked and bit her bottom lip. 'If you could come down, that would be much appreciated. My neck is killing me from looking at you.'

'Fine, I'm coming,' she said as she closed the doors to her balcony.

She was nervous, although the predominate feeling was anticipation. Meeting someone's family was a sign of permanence. Obviously, he wanted her in his life, or they wouldn't be standing on his veranda ready to meet his mother. Things had moved fairly quickly between the two of them. When Vivienne wasn't spending time alone, she was either with Amelie or Adrion. They had become a place of comfort. She liked being able to invest time in a few relationships, rather than trying to maintain many. It confused her why some people were obsessed with popularity. Sounded like a chore above anything else. How could someone have possibly had meaningful relationships with more than a dozen people? She could count her relationships on one hand. Adrion, Amelie, Marion, Louis, and Bonnie. Vivienne wondered if she had fallen in love with Adrion. It was hard to know what love felt like. She didn't want to misdiagnose it.

'Now, don't stress—you're going to be great,' Adrion said as he wrapped his arm around her shoulder.

'I know.' Before they had even knocked, the door started to open.

Adrion's mother sauntered out. 'Vivienne,' she said, gently cupping Vivienne's cheek in her hand. 'I'm Sofia. It's so nice to finally be able to meet you.' Adrion and his mother locked eyes. 'Your description didn't do her justice—look how sweet she is. Look at those legs. You could be a model, for God's sake.' Her smile grew bigger as she swayed her attention back to Vivienne.

She wasn't expecting to meet someone so exuberant. It was

a relief, actually, but she was also lost for words. 'Thank you. You also look fantastic.'

'You know what the secret is? Adding spinach into your diet. Trust me, it works miracles for the skin.'

'Okay, that's enough, Mum,' Adrion interrupted teasingly.

'Come in, take a seat wherever you like. I prepared us cannelloni for dinner. It's Nonna's old recipe.' Vivienne pulled out a chair and sat down. The place was homely, packed with big leafy plants and scattered with family photos. None with Adrion's father. He never talked about him. She assumed it might have been a touchy subject and respected boundaries. Even though her curiosity usually knew no bounds. He had spoken about his cousins before, though. Most of them lived in Italy. He and Sofia would visit them during the break. They still owned their old family home down there.

'How's university, Vivienne? I heard you're studying literature, is that right?' Sofia asked. Her voice was rich and husky. It was almost seductive to listen to.

'University is going really well, actually. I'm finding my job at the publisher has helped with my writing immensely.'

'Adrion mentioned your work. I think it's fantastic that young people such as yourself are able to have opportunities like this.' She continued, 'When I was your age, I could have only dreamt of securing a job like that. I got my first job when I was twenty-five and lived with my parents until I was thirty. What a mistake that was.' Sofia managed a successful flower shop in the centre of Les Halles. Many of their customers were tourists who would stumble by after a day of indulging in expensive gifts and souvenirs. She also created beautiful flower arrangements for weddings and other functions, which she considered the highlight of her job.

Adrion sat up from the table and assisted his mother with the tray of cannelloni.

'That smells delicious.' The smell hadn't reached her, but she knew there was no harm in being polite.

'Trust me, it tastes even better,' Adrion said, pouring a generous amount of red wine into everyone's glass.

Dinner was accompanied with embarrassing childhood stories and Adrion frantically diverting the conversation. When he finally realised his mum wouldn't stop sabotaging him, he began telling embarrassing stories of her. It was amusing to see how animated Adrion became around Sofia. He felt like a completely different person. The connection he had with Sofia reminded her of her own relationship with Marion. It reminded her how much they used to laugh. It reminded her how cancer took that away.

'Do you have any plans for the holidays?' Sofia asked, ever so faintly slurring her words. She was considerably more intoxicated than Vivienne and Adrion, even though the three of them had all had similar amounts to drink. Sofia was even more cheerful drunk, though Vivienne questioned how that was possible.

'The friend I mentioned, Amelie, she has a place near the Loire Valley. We might go down for a few weeks.'

'Good, it's nice to get away. Adrion and I are going to go visit our relatives in Italy over the summer.' Sofia took another sip of her wine and swallowed abruptly, as if she'd had an epiphany. 'You know what? You should come with us.' Vivienne didn't know if this was a real invite or the wine speaking. She turned and faced Adrion next to her and he exchanged a nod of approval.

'I'll let you two discuss it, but I would love for you to come.'

Adrion took his plate and glass of wine and placed it in the sink. 'Thanks for dinner, Mum. I think Vivienne and I are going to head back to hers for the night.'

Sofia sighed. 'Okay, love.' Gazing into her eyes, it was obvious that she missed her youth.

'See? My mum loved you,' Adrion said in a low voice, as Sofia waved from the front door.

'So, Italy.'

'I think you should come. It'd be fun.'

Vivienne fastened her seatbelt and pulled her hair into a tight bun. She pressed her lips together and smiled. 'I'll sleep on it.'

They arrived back at the apartment just before midnight. After fumbling with the key, she finally managed to slide it through the hole and unlock the door. She attempted to unzip her dress, but she was too drunk and unable to reach. Adrion saw her struggling and crept up to help. His fingers were smooth like polished wood. His chest pressed against her bare back as she slipped off the dress. Vivienne could feel her pulse quicken. Adrion's hands moved further. Waist, then hips. His warm breath made the hairs on her neck erect. She had never had sex before. Sometimes she thought she had fallen behind, that she was too sexually inexperienced and therefore undesirable. She hadn't lost her virginity—not because she was frigid or waiting for marriage, but because she had romanticised it to a point where she wouldn't settle for anything less than perfect. But she could no longer resist the taste of Adrion's neck. Taking his hand, she guided it around her thigh until it reached her underwear. She wanted him badly, and she was finally ready.

CHAPTER EIGHT

Pen to paper. Professor Clarke was right. The beige book lay empty on the desk, the lines unoccupied. For a place where ideas were supposed to be born, the pages were arid. Without words, paper was simply dead trees, and Vivienne couldn't condone that level of slaughter. Not without a cause. She slid the drawer open, removed the bottle of bourbon, and poured the equivalent of three shots into her glass. People were capable of such complex thoughts and ideas. It perplexed Vivienne how she had the capacity to feel love, prejudice, and desire. There were other emotions to consider, however these were the first that came to her mind. She remembered attending a funeral once. The person who had passed was a close family friend of her mother. Her name escaped Vivienne. Everybody attending uncontrollably cried as the casket left the church and their relatives read eulogies. She was young as well—in her forties—and the death was unexpected.

Vivienne saw the body before it was buried and even touched it when nobody was looking. The skin was cold and stuck to her fingers like glue. Then she waited a few seconds to make sure the body didn't move or open its eyes. Her own death didn't scare her. That day made it look peaceful. Quiet after a storm. Then three days later, she was walking home from school and tripped over a dead Labrador lying on the side of the road. She rolled it away from the gutter and waved the flies away from the body. Lion, the name tag said. Vivienne's throat started to close over, and she couldn't see through the thick barrier of unreleased tears. She sat next to the dog for almost an hour, patting its head. The situation proved to her how out of tune she was with her own emotions. Not a single tear was shed for a family who had lost a mother, a wife. Yet this mutt made her want to curl up and lie in the gutter as well. Maybe it was the purity or innocence of the dog. Maybe it was because she realised death disregarded justice.

Vivienne dragged the notepad towards her and gulped the last of her drink. She shook her hands, cracked her neck, and grabbed the pen. It was still unknown exactly what she was about to write, but she knew that the pen had to touch the paper at some point. She wanted to write about love. She thought for a second. Love always paired nicely with injustice. Vivienne hated books where the protagonists achieved everything they wanted. The idea of 'happily ever after' was an unrealistic trope. She wanted her writing to involve tragedy and loss. A story where the reader would be left in the dark. How she loved dramatic irony—she'd have bathed in it if she could. She wanted her audience to understand the characters, but at the same time absolutely despise them. That was an area in which she could excel. She wanted people's guts to wrench whilst they read. It had to be intense and show stopping.

Her thoughts were interrupted by an unexpected epiphany. Her pen finally marked the paper. A single line stained the pages. It read, 'Two lovers, set to kill each other out of uncontrollable jealousy and lust. One succeeds.' The page laid there flat as she analysed it. She may as well have just written the plot of every Shakespeare play—ever. But it was an idea, nonetheless. Sometimes, a simple idea had the ability to spark a revolution of thoughts. She needed an outlet. A sense of purpose. Maybe vicariously living through the characters she created could give her that. Vivienne continued to write lines of nonsensical notes that, in her mind, made complete sense. She could feel a story trying to push its way out of her brain.

One o'clock in the morning struck and she was struggling to keep her eyes open. Work was still a duty she had to fulfil the next morning. Her bed sat there, inviting her in, and within minutes, she was out cold.

Vivienne raced into the office, placing a coffee on Hugo's desk.

'Thanks, Viv.'

'Don't mention it,' she said, inching towards the door.

'We have a new potential client. She wants to meet today, but my hands are tied. Do you think you're ready to scout this one out by yourself?'

'Hugo, I was born ready. You can trust me.' It was paramount that she secured this client. Hugo's faith and her reputation depended on it.

'Also, just between us, we're down in business.'

Vivienne sat in the chair across from him. 'How's that possible? Two months ago was the busiest we had been in ages.'

'It's fucking Reed's. They've opened up a few blocks down. I'm trying to avoid telling everyone. I don't need the mass hysteria.' Reed's was bad news. They were a new, flashy publisher that originated in the U.S a few years back, however, they had managed to sink their teeth into the French market. Anyone who wanted to be *anyone* tried to get their book signed with them.

'What can we do about it?'

'Nothing. Business as usual, I suppose. We just have to up our game and not let clients slip.' At the end of the day, they had the lay of the land and thirty-three years of experience and trust under their belt.

'What's her name?'

'Whose?'

Vivienne frowned. 'The client.'

'Oh right. Caroline. We go way back. You'll like her, I reckon.'

The client Vivienne was supposed to meet was named Caroline Babin. She had published three books over her life, two of those with Hugo and the company. Vivienne had read one of her books out of pure chance. It was about the suffragette movement in the early 1910s. Riveting stuff.

Vivienne entered the café and looked around for someone who matched Hugo's vague description. 'Hi, Caroline Babin?' she said, as she slid into the booth.

'Yes?'

'I'm Vivienne, I work for Hugo. I'm here to discuss your book.'

'Oh, I was expecting Hugo.' Caroline looked around the shop, lost, creating an overwhelming awkwardness.

'He was tied up at the office. But trust me, I can do the job better.'

Caroline eased her posture and cleansed the room with a slight side smile. 'Alright then, let's proceed. I have a few things I want to discuss.'

'Shoot.'

Caroline brought out a large book with notes and fabric hanging from the side—the kind of book Vivienne imagined a cliché witch would carry with them. Caroline began to set out her demands, which included minimal changes to the story line, explaining the pieces that couldn't be altered because she thought they would lose their 'authenticity'.

'I'll run it past Hugo,' Vivienne kept on saying, not sure how else to respond.

Out also fell a few illustration ideas that she was eager

to share. Although, that wasn't Vivienne's area of expertise. Caroline didn't mind though and showed her anyway, which took the better half of twenty minutes.

Caroline opened her large woven bag, pulling out a second manuscript, and handed it to Vivienne. As Vivienne went to take it, she stopped her. 'What about you?'

'Pardon?' she responded.

'What about you? You write?'

It was unclear why this woman she had met less than forty minutes ago was asking her such a question. She had started last night; did that count? 'Trying to.'

'I can sense energies and yours is really standing out. You seem to have a good head on those shoulders.' Vivienne looked at her blankly, unable to respond. She was flattered, but that didn't change the fact that she thought Caroline was a little off her rocker. 'Well, I won't keep you, you're probably very busy.'

'Thank you for your time, Caroline. I look forward to reading the manuscript and working with you down the line.'

Soon after, she left the restaurant and drove back to the company, impressed with herself. Hugo was delighted to hear that Caroline had agreed to work with them once again. It was obvious Vivienne was now becoming his knight in shining armour.

Seven thousand one hundred and thirty-nine. That was the number of languages that had existed. Seven thousand one hundred and thirty-nine ways to say I love you. Or I hate you. Of course, not every word could be translated perfectly into each language. But they could be abstracted into a form that every tongue could understand. One hundred and fifty thousand years was how long language had graced the Earth. Humans had worked their way to the top, from casual grunts to landing on the moon. It was difficult to fathom the progression of mankind. Nurture or nature? Vivienne contemplated the question a lot. When a person was born, were their personality, thoughts, and future predetermined, or were all humans a product of their environment? She always had a challenging relationship with fate. She didn't know whether something almighty and powerful had paved her life with yellow bricks or whether she made her own destiny. Her parents were Catholic, however, they rarely attended church. They had inherited their beliefs from their parents. Deep down, she knew that they didn't truly believe in a God. Vivienne did believe in something, though. It may not have been a well-renowned religion, but she thought there was a possibility of something beyond her life, a place where the soul awaited to be reborn. She viewed religion as a method to control and manipulate people. This wasn't to say that she didn't respect it—some people truly did find enlightenment, and she was happy for them. What didn't sit easily with her was the thought of people carrying out their lives only to please an almighty presence.

All she knew now was that she did in fact create her own fate, regardless of anyone or anything. Pen was once more on paper. Again, she found herself reminded of what she set out to achieve. It had to reflect her, no matter how unsavoury. Hundreds of books she had read over her lifetime, but very few made a home in her memory. She wanted something that stuck, something that screamed Vivienne Larue. She reached over and dragged the off-white typewriter towards her. The beige booklet now containing various notes laid next to her. As her finger hit the first key, not only was it the beginning of a story, but also the beginning of a prolonged dream.

CHAPTER NINE

Adrion reached into his pocket. A packet of cigarettes appeared in his palm. He dug deeper and pulled out a lighter, and after three strikes, the flame popped to the surface.

'Here.' He gestured to the cigarette as he exhaled.

'Thanks.' After one big hit, Vivienne passed it back to him. Both of them waited patiently, seated in the terminal. They had barely arrived on time, after a quick lunch break led to spilled coffee and soaked luggage. Adrion could be extremely clumsy occasionally. It would usually compound, and the incident on the way to the airport was no exception. Firstly, he spilt a small drop, which he unsuccessfully tried to lick off himself. Then, when placing his arm back down, his elbow rapidly swung and hit the mug, ending in a suitcase saturated in coffee. It was like watching a dog chase its own tail.

'That's a lot of books you brought.'

'Yeah, well, I don't want to get bored, now do I?' Vivienne said with a smug look.

'If our plane goes down, I'm blaming you.'

'If our plane goes down, it's probably because you touched something you weren't supposed to. Thank God you're not a pilot, you'd be knocking things left, right, and centre. You would kill everybody.' She lowered her voice and returned to her book.

Adrion took her hand and bit it playfully. 'I'm glad you agreed to come.'

Vivienne was in two minds whether to accept the invite to Italy. There was slight hesitation when she agreed originally. Her mother needed her, but Marion refused to let Vivienne turn down the opportunity. Three weeks was a long time to be away from her. Too long. The second reason was that she missed Amelie. They had drifted, and Vivienne had noticed that she was preoccupied with other 'things'. That's how Amelie described it—she had other 'things' going on. Vivienne wished she knew why she had been so distant. Her relationship with Adrion was very time consuming, so the thoughts of Amelie were often fleeting.

'I'm happy I came.'

'Viv, you're going to love Turin. Relax all day, party all night.'

She had seen pictures of when he had been there last. Italy was beautiful. She had gone to the Amalfi Coast with her parents when she was younger. Nothing but clear ocean and colourful houses for miles. She fell asleep on the beach one day and was sunburnt to the point that she couldn't get out of bed. She always forgot the sun could do that.

'I was jealous when you showed me the photos.'

'The photos don't do it justice. You simply fall in love when you see the place in person.' Adrion pushed his cigarette into the ashtray and picked up his carry-on bag. They arrived at the gate, where an airhostess punched two holes into their tickets and pointed them to their seats. It had been a while since Vivienne had flown. Five years almost. The strange bursting sensation in her ears made her so nauseous that she dreaded the thought of flying. Marion always stocked up on vomit bags before they boarded.

Although, their flight to Turin had been quick, and Vivienne had avoided vomiting. They picked up their suitcases and walked to the front of the airport, where Sofia leant against her car, waiting. 'You made it. Here, let me take your stuff,' she said, kissing them on either cheek. Sofia had decided to come down a few weeks earlier. Adrion had mentioned that she had felt homesick and needed to surround herself with familiar faces.

'How is everyone, Mum?'

'The usual. They're good. Very excited to meet your girlfriend.'

'We won't be staying long. We have a big night planned.'

'We do?' Vivienne interrupted. A day of rest would have been nice before leaping into the action.

'I mean, there's no time to waste, right?'

'I suppose.'

As they entered the city, 18th-century homes filled the stone-paved streets. There was a large open space with a statue in the centre of it. Adrion had explained who he was, but she had forgotten. After driving to the edge of the town, the car came to a halt. Outside was a three-storey house with off-white walls and terracotta roofing. It was identical to the ones that she had seen in the centre of town but had clearly been refurbished or renovated. Sofia rummaged through her bag for the keys and unlocked the door.

Heads started to appear from every crevice as they entered. First the stairs, then the kitchen. 'Is that Vivienne?' a voice whispered. Ten sets of eyes stared at her. Vivienne felt like an animal in a zoo. As if she was expected to do a trick. It was intimidating, but one by one, they came up to her and introduced themselves. One of Adrion's older cousins told her that he had never brought a girl home before, and that was the reason for their excitement. It pleased her to know that she was the first to pin him down.

The evening had started to dawn upon them, and it was clear that Adrion was eager to explore the town.

'Where do you want to go tonight?'

'You're the local here, you tell me.'

'Okay, I know a place.' Her keen eye had noticed that he had a habit of saying that. However, when he said he 'knew a place', he certainly meant it. Adrion grabbed her hand and quickly bolted out the front door. His family indistinctively whispered and laughed from the back room. She felt truly alive with him. He was like a pump of adrenaline after an anaphylactic shock. They ran down the city's streets and her past flashed before her. The childhood she was never fully satisfied with. Her inability to form meaningful relationships. Vivienne hoped that if her younger self could see her, she would have been proud of the life she'd started to build. Proud of the person she was becoming. She had read so many books about love, waiting patiently for the day she would finally experience it. She used to wonder if it would ever arrive. But it had. Vivienne had everything she wanted, and she could almost see it too.

Adrion turned sharply to his left and entered a neat little bar, tucked away from the busy streets. 'We're here.'

'A bar.' A bar was something that would never disappoint her.

'Yes, a bar, Viv. Now get over here.' He pulled out a stool and sat at the counter. 'I'll have a single malt Scotch,' he yelled, waving down a bartender. 'What would you like?'

'I'll have the same as you.' Adrion passed her an odd look. 'What's that look?'

'I don't know, I just never figured you to be a Scotch girl. You seem like a margarita girl.' It was clear he was pulling her leg, but she decided to play along with his games.

'And what makes you say that?'

'It's just not very lady like.' He smiled, knowing she was getting riled up.

'I'll show you how lady like I can be.' Her hand shot up. 'I'll have a Scotch. And make it a double.' The bartender nodded from the end of the bar.

'I see you.' Adrion nodded, downing his first glass.

'I'll outdrink you any day.'

'Is that right?' He laughed. 'You're on.'

This was a challenge Vivienne knew she could win—her tolerance of alcohol was incredibly high. A blessing or a curse, it was undecided. Her wallet would've argued a curse. At the fifth drink, Adrion was up on the bar, dancing to the live band. By the sixth, walking had become a challenge, and dancing was out of the picture.

It was hard to understand what he was saying over the music. Or maybe she was too drunk to comprehend his words. They were entering one ear and getting lost somewhere in transit. Then there was an abrupt break in the music.

'Adrion, let's go.' They both snuck out of the bar, forgetting to pay for their last drink.

'I think we should get gelato.'

'I could really go for some gelato.' They both laughed and stumbled down the street, their nonsensical talk suddenly disrupted by a crunching sound. Adrion toppled to the ground, dragging Vivienne with him. The grazes on their shins were met with more uncontrollable laughter. Both of them laid down, too out of breath to stand up.

They rested in the dark alley and gazed to the sky, the moon watching over them.

'Adrion . . . I love you.' The three words rang though the air, like the final note of a grand symphony. It echoed, and for a split second, he was the only thing that existed in her mind. The only thing that mattered. The words hadn't been forced or coerced in any way. This was as pure and as raw as they came. Her heart had been elusive, but now it was officially on her sleeve for everyone to see. He had caught it.

'Vivienne . . . I love you too.' The words were sickening in the best way possible. They stopped and stared at each other for assurance. 'Let's go get our gelato, shall we?'

Everything felt euphoric.

After ten minutes of waiting, Adrion finally decided on a flavour. All that time standing there just for him to pick chocolate. He then stole Vivienne's cup and took a big spoon of her gelato.

'What is this?' he said, as he scrunched his nose and scraped his tongue against his teeth.

'It's liquorice.'

'Interesting.'

'It's my father's favourite flavour,' she justified. They crouched on the edge of the canal, with their feet hanging a few centimetres above the water. 'Every time we went out to get ice cream, he would only get liquorice, never anything different. He was always like that, found something good and stuck to it.'

'So why do you get that flavour?' Vivienne looked at her distorted figure in the water, then brought her attention back to Adrion.

'I suppose it reminds me of him. And the good times.' When she focused on preventing the drops of creamy bliss from running down the cone, it was as if time stopped. The simplicity of savouring the flavours distracted her from her mind that was always spinning. And when she got liquorice, the taste transported her into the arms of her father.

'What about your dad?' As it rolled from her tongue, a cloud of instant regret casted upon her. Was she really that insensitive? Adrion laughed nasally, and his head sank. 'Sorry.' She put her hand on his thigh.

'No, it's okay, don't apologise. It's just hard to talk about him.'

'You don't have to if you don't want to.'

'No, I want to.' He inhaled and sighed. 'I was eleven. Mum and Dad fought constantly, but one day, I heard my mum ripping into him. He was having an affair, but I was too young to understand at the time. Then three weeks later, he contracted pneumonia and went into multi-organ failure. Soon after, he died, just like that.' Adrion's voice started to tremble, his eyes red, and tone indistinguishable from sadness or anger. 'He left me twice in my life. Once when he abandoned our family. Once when he passed. It's sad to think that in his final hours, the only people he had around him were those he deserted. Mum wouldn't get out of bed for months. She blamed herself for his death.' Vivienne knew his father was no longer in his life, but she didn't realise he was dead. She could hear from his tone that the wound had never been truly healed, and that he had carried the burden for a long time. 'I've never told anyone that before.'

Vivienne turned him towards her. All she wanted to do was strip him of his pain. 'I'm sorry. You didn't deserve that.' Tears glazed her eyes.

'Please don't cry, Vivienne. I'm fine,' he said, wiping away the tears that ran along his nose. She hadn't told him about her mother's cancer. But with love came trust, and love was a word she couldn't take back.

'Adrion, my mother has cancer. That was the reason I kept shutting down the idea of meeting her.' Vivienne's strong façade crumbled. At least now she had someone who could help her feel whole again. He didn't say anything—he knew that words couldn't do much.

She dragged her feet along the ash grey sand, and the rugged cliffs started to collapse around her. She shook as the water washed over her feet. *Further,* a voice said. Then there was a drop. Vivienne looked down to see a black abyss consume her. The waves began to topple over her, each breath becoming increasingly more difficult. She screamed for help, but it was as if there was no air within her lungs, then everything turned pitch black. She gasped, her forehead was polished with sweat, and her pillow was damp. In a haze, she stood up from the bed and wandered down the hall. She opened a door, expecting to see the bathroom, but instead, sitting there was Emma.

'This isn't the bathroom,' Vivienne said, disoriented.

'No this is definitely *not* the bathroom.'

'Sorry.' The door slowly closed, but before it shut, Emma swiftly stood up and tugged it wide open.

'Hey, come sit. You look like you've seen a ghost.'

'Yeah, I had a really odd dream.'

'There is so much to be said about dreams. What was yours about?' Emma was one of Adrion's cousins. Out of everyone in his family, Vivienne took a particular liking to her. She was more introverted than the others, but effortless to converse with. And well read.

'I've had this dream before.' Sitting next to Emma, she started to explain. 'I'm on this beach with dark sand, and these cliffs are falling around me. My only choice is to go into the water, but when I do, waves topple over me, and I'm trapped. I scream for help, but nothing comes out. Then everything turns black.'

'Interesting. I read that drowning in a dream can mean rebirth. Or a struggle, perhaps. Maybe you feel trapped or caged in your life. Maybe you're trying to avoid facing your struggles . . . or maybe they're just beginning.' Vivienne didn't believe in superstition. Dreams were just a manifestation of random thoughts. They didn't really have the ability to warn.

'Who knows.'

'You know, Adrion's always been a happy person, full to the brim with joy. But when you're around, his smile reaches his ears. I see the way he looks at you. Like you're a diamond.' It felt nice to know that someone other than herself saw the connection between them. She didn't need affirmation from anyone to validate their relationship. Yet it was nice that someone did.

'I'm not as shiny as a diamond, but thank you.'

'None of us are shiny. All of us have been dulled at some point in our life. The most beautiful things have usually undergone changes. Diamonds form under pressure.' The conversation fell silent momentarily. Emma pulled out a photo from one of her drawers and gazed at it pensively. 'My father was a drunk and my mother tried her best to raise me. Though she didn't have a motherly bone in her body. Growing up, I was jealous of my cousin's family. Such an ugly thing to admit.' She placed the photo down. 'When I learnt about what had happened to Adrion's father, it put things into perspective for me. That it doesn't matter who you are, bad things can and will happen to you. Instead of being resentful, I integrated into my extended family. These are my people. Not my unfortunate past.' Emma was right. Blood didn't define a person's family.

'I wish we met sooner.'

'I know, you're like the sister I never had. Call me from Paris though, we should keep in touch.' Emma got up from the bed and opened her closet. 'I should get dressed for dinner, give you and Adrion a nice send-off.' A sigh left her mouth as she slid the coat hangers across the metal bar, trying to find something suitable to wear.

'We'll return. Turin feels like home.' Vivienne turned her back to Emma and twisted the doorknob.

'Oh, and also, the incident with Adrion's father really impacted him, even though he hides it well. There's more to him than just charm. He's got a good heart, but he finds it hard to fully trust. I suppose it's to protect himself if someone leaves.'

Vivienne thought carefully about a response. 'I don't plan on leaving.' She didn't know if Emma was trying to insinuate something, but it stuck. *None of us are shiny.* She quickly wrote it in her journal when she returned to her room.

The glasses clinked together. The feast was massive, on par

with the ones that Marion would host for family gatherings. It was like a modern-day last supper, except no one was going to end up crucified on a cross afterwards. Adrion and Vivienne left the dinner early, hoping to get some rest before their morning flight.

CHAPTER TEN

'Thanks for taking her.' Vivienne grabbed Bonnie from the floor as she pranced out of Chloe's apartment.

'Of course. You're such a good girl, aren't you?' Chloe reached for the cat's face and grabbed it.

'I owe you one.'

'Don't be silly. You enjoy your trip?'

'Turin was beautiful.' When she said the word aloud, she could feel the warmth of the town and the joy on Adrion's face. 'I have a gift for Amelie that I'm going to pop over and give her. She loves tea so I got her a tea pot.' It was a grey, ceramic pot, moulded into the shape of a crow. She had stumbled across it in town, where an old lady was selling them out of her car. It had Amelie's name written all over it.

'A lovely gift. I don't want to keep you. Do you want to have coffee when you're back and talk more?' Chloe said, patting Bonnie's head again.

'Would love to.'

Vivienne walked up the seven marble steps, like she had countless times before, and rang the doorbell.

Amelie poked her head out. 'Vivienne?'

She barged in without replying. 'Amelie, Turin was amazing. The city had the most breath-taking buildings. You should have seen them, they would have been right up your alley. Also, I got you this.' Vivienne handed her the box containing the gift and walked to the lounge room. Suddenly, a man with ruffed-up hair and an undone button-up shirt appeared.

'Amelie, who's this?'

'No one,' she said frantically. The atmosphere became so tense a knife could cut through it.

Vivienne scanned him from head to toe. 'You're sleeping with him. Aren't you?'

'Actually, we're dating,' the man corrected her. 'My name's Jac, by the way.'

'I'm sorry, how long have you two been . . . a thing?'

'About two months.'

'Closer to three,' Jac corrected her, once again interrupting. Vivienne had been seeing Adrion for over half a year and Amelie had known about it from the very beginning. But *she* had the audacity to hide this from her for three entire months.

Vivienne's tone became hostile. 'You've been keeping this from me for that long? Were you planning on telling me?'

'It hadn't been official, please don't get mad.' How could she tell her not to be mad? Their friendship was the ride-or-die kind, the type of friendship built on trust. Amelie had broken that trust.

'How could you not say anything? I can't believe this is what you've been so busy with. I always tell you absolutely everything.'

'I think you're overreacting.' She gestured Jac towards the front door and whispered. 'You should leave.'

'Yes. I think you should leave, Jac.' There was a noticeable emphasis on 'leave' and 'Jac'. 'And no, Amelie, I don't think I am overreacting, quite frankly.'

'What? So you're the only one who's allowed to be happy? It's always all about you. Never about me.' Amelie's voice rung with aggression.

'That's so unfair.'

'Is it? Because I think I deserve to be happy too.'

'Who the fuck said you didn't deserve to be happy? You're pulling things out of your arse now.'

'Why do you feel the need to be such bitch?' Every syllable she pronounced filled with anger.

'Because I come over to tell you about my trip where I confessed my love for Adrion, and I find out that you have been ignoring me for some pathetic man. I'm mad because you lied to my face.'

'Well, not everyone can have your perfect little life, can they?'

'Me. Perfect life? Amelie, look where you live—spare me.'

'Oh, so this is a money thing now, is it?'

'Maybe, yeah. If you hadn't been ignoring me so much you might have known that I barely had enough money for rent last month. Not to mention my parents are drowning in bills for Marion's cancer treatment.'

'Marion has cancer?' Her tone dulled as the realisation sank in. Guilt had set upon her, before the flame of anger quickly reignited.

'Yes, Amelie, she does. And they say she's getting better, but who fucking knows.'

'I'm sorry, okay? But you don't have the right to barge into my house and accuse me of such unreasonable things. I'm still struggling, and I still feel like I'm suffocating. Just because our problems are different doesn't invalidate what *I'm* going through,' she said, out of breath. Tears in her eyes started to form.

Vivienne knew Amelie had a point. Shouting and yelling wasn't going to benefit either of them, though. Vivienne grabbed her bag and stormed out without another word. As she raced down the seven marble steps, tears gushed down her cheeks. She was enraged, but she was also ashamed. Because deep down, she knew she was no better than Amelie.

CHAPTER ELEVEN

There was radio silence. Neither had reached out, and it was likely that neither would've. The only time they had seen each other was at the university. Even then, the looks were cold and unforgiving. Vivienne had never imagined fighting with Amelie. Until now, they had never had anything to fight about. And of course, it was over some man. She didn't approve of Amelie and Jac's relationship, and she never would. There was an uncanny look about him, as if he were hiding something behind those thick eyebrows and dark black beard. He was attractive, and Vivienne could see why someone like Amelie would've fallen for him. However, in her mind, he was the ugliest thing to ever crawl the Earth. He was a parasite that had infected their relationship. The fight constantly played in her mind like a broken record. She was someone who prided herself on being rational and not letting her emotions consume her, but how she had acted had been so childish. Adrion had told her not to do anything crazy and let the waters calm. One fight wouldn't destroy their entire friendship, and if it could, then maybe their friendship wasn't as sturdy as she thought it was. She wanted to tell Amelie about Turin. About how the trip had made her feel complete. But it was all ruined now.

'I made us dinner.'

Vivienne rolled to her side and looked at Marion. 'I'm not hungry.'

'We can sit outside, it'll be nice.'

'Alright, I'll be down in a second.' She placed the book on her bedside table and slipped her feet into the shoes next to her bed.

The apartment had made her feel alone. Alone was too kind of a word; she liked being alone. What she had really felt was isolated. Her plants had started to wilt and die because watering them felt like a chore. Everything had felt like a chore. She needed to escape, but unfortunately even death lingered where she hoped to seek refuge.

'I'm glad you decided to come home for a bit. That apartment's not good, you need to be with your family.' Marion passed her a plate of salmon, which had been placed on bed of sautéed mushrooms and spinach. 'I know you don't want to talk about Amelie, but I'm here to listen.' She poured the warm jus from the pan onto the plate. 'I'm a good listener, you know that.' A smile crossed her face, attempting to inject some life into the room.

'I'll tell you as long as you don't give me advice.'

'I'm just ears.'

They walked with their plates to the tree in the backyard, which had a white iron table and matching chairs. As a child, Vivienne would always sit under the tree and read. It also used to have a makeshift swing made out of rope and timber that hung from one of the branches. Her parents took it down when she was thirteen. She swung too far up, and the rope chafed and snapped. A fractured ankle permanently ended the fun. She remembered the sensation of the ground hitting her, surprised that she hadn't done more damage. Especially at that age, she was more bones than anything else. It wasn't the fractured ankle that had caused the most pain, but the fact that she could no longer ride her bicycle with Thomas. He still made sure to come to her house every day and bring chocolates to cheer her up—even though he ended up eating most of them. He also offered to stick his hand down her cast to massage and scratch her leg, which she never denied. After the cast came off—which had felt like a lifetime—she could barely contain her excitement. When she got back from the hospital, Thomas was standing outside her house with his bicycle in one hand and hers in the other. It trumped any birthday or Christmas present she could've ever imagined.

Vivienne explained the details of the fight. There was no such thing as oversharing when it came to talking with her mother. Marion—although unsolicited—repeated the same thing Adrion told her. 'Give the situation time to settle,' she had said. Marion added that it would take less time if Vivienne reached out first. That wasn't going to happen. It may have been her stubbornness, or the fear of her apology being rejected. Whatever it was, she simply couldn't do it. The looks Amelie had been giving in class hadn't exactly screamed 'come over for dinner and wine and we can sort things out'. Camping out with her parents was not a solution—eventually, she was going to have to face her. As well as Hugo, who would've undoubtably been annoyed about all the 'sick' days she had taken.

'I think I'll go back tomorrow. Have to face the music eventually.' Vivienne placed her dish in the sink and ran some hot water over it. 'Plus, it's such a hassle to get to the university every day from here. The petrol is going to cost me more than my rent.'

'Maybe you could cut costs by coming back home.' Marion glanced up at Vivienne. She always had a hidden agenda. 'I hope you and Amelie manage to sort this out.' Her arms reached out with reassurance.

'I'm going to have an early night. Say hello to Dad for me when he's back from work,' Vivienne said, her voice slightly muffled from the hug. She walked up the stairs and Marion watched from behind.

'Also, don't forget we have an appointment with Dr Dupont on Tuesday. 10 o'clock.' Vivienne had missed the last appointment because of work but had promised Marion—and herself—that she wouldn't miss another again.

The perpetual glare became less frequent. Amelie seemed fatigued and her skin pale. She was most likely sick. There was no doubt in Vivienne's mind that once she was better, the grim looks would've continued. Ignoring one another had become tedious, and she was experiencing the full brunt of it now. Over the course of three nights, she considered calling Amelie sixteen times. Out of those sixteen times, she began dialling the numbers twice, losing motivation halfway through both. Once again, she was arriving home without her partner in crime. Her Bonnie. Or Clyde. It didn't matter which one she was in the scenario, she just wanted Amelie back.

Vivienne unpacked the fresh pasta she had picked up on the way home and waited as the half-filled pot boiled. Every time she imagined the phone, it inched closer to her. And so did the overwhelming urge to call Amelie. One foot in front of the other, she arrived at the phone and stared down at it. Her index finger began to dial the numbers. Third time lucky.

Before she could enter the last digit, there was a dreary thump at the door. She hesitantly placed down the phone. It was probably Chloe asking for another bag of flour. She always accommodated her because she knew she would reap the rewards later. The pastries were simply mouth-watering. The idea of the polite encounter was crushed, and instead, Amelie stood in front of her. But not the Amelie she'd once known. Her right eye was bruised, cheek swollen, and her mascara ran down her face like a stream of distress. She collapsed into Vivienne's arms. It wasn't a graceful fall, like the type where all is forgiven.

This was a fall for help. Amelie looked up at Vivienne, shell-shocked, like someone had been dismembered right in front of her and she'd been forced to watch. Vivienne stood there confused—no contact for weeks and then *this*. Just because they were in the midst of a feud didn't mean she stopped caring for her. As soon as Amelie stepped through the threshold of those doors, everything had been placed on hold. Vivienne tried to calm her hysterical crying, while Amelie frantically attempted to explain what had happened. Yet every time she spoke, only staggered, unidentifiable noises drifted out. Vivienne raced to the kitchen and took a box of tissues. She rubbed the mascara off Amelie's undereye, then wiped the tears that had combined with her runny nose, forming a wet, snotty mess on her upper lip. Wrapping her arms around Amelie's head, she stroked her, starting from the scalp and moving towards the fifth vertebrae, continuing the pattern.

The pot on the stove, left unattended, started to overflow. 'You don't have to talk. Only when you're ready. But remember, I'm here.' She lowered the pasta into the pot and walked back to the couch. Amelie buried her face into her knees. 'And I'm sorry.' Vivienne added.

Amelie sat on the couch for hours and said nothing. Vivienne cooked her dinner, poured some sparkling water into her glass, and made sure she was comfortable. She attempted to type a few pages of her novel, but her shadow's presence was too distracting. Eventually, Amelie arose from her depressive haze and meandered to the desk, holding two glasses of water. Some colour had returned to her cheeks, and her ghostly expression started to fade. She dragged a stool, sat next to Vivienne, and tilted her head as if she was trying to read the notes. 'What are you writing?' she said in a monotone voice.

'Just notes for my novel.'

'You're writing a novel?'

She had forgotten that she hadn't told Amelie about her writing. So much for telling each other everything. 'Yeah, it's not a lot at the moment. I've done the first three chapters. I'm still trying to figure where I want the story to go.'

Amelie took a big sip from her glass and groaned. 'Can I explain?' She pointed in a circular motion to her face.

'Yes. I'll just sit and listen.'

Amelie closed her eyes and looked down into her lap, in an attempt to conceal her uncomfortable expression. 'You know the bistro that we went to a while back. Bagatelle?' Vivienne nodded her head up and down, making sure not to interrupt. She didn't really want the long-winded recount of events, she just wanted to confirm her suspicions—that this pain inflicted on Amelie was indeed by Jac's hand. 'He was waiting tables there that night, and when you were outside waiting for me to pay, he slipped me a note with his phone number. We had been giving each other looks throughout the night, but I didn't expect anything to come of it.' There was a vague memory Vivienne recollected from that night, of Amelie grinning at a piece of paper and slipping it into her purse, not realising at the time it was the beginning of a secret romance that would take place right under her nose.

'I went over to his place for drinks a few days later and then things progressed from there. I wanted to tell you about the relationship, but he told me not to.' Amelie rubbed her eyes then bit her nails, which were jagged and uneven. It was an awful habit, but one that stemmed from some form of undiagnosed anxiety.

She tore a piece of nail from her thumb and resumed. 'He always wanted to have sex, which was fine for a while, don't get me wrong. But it became exhausting, like a chore. I just wanted to do things that normal couples did. I never verbally said no to sex, but in my head, I thought, why am I doing this to myself?

When you came back from your trip, it made me realise I was perusing something that simply wasn't there. I long for something like what you and Adrion have. Instead, I got this crap.'

'So, what happened to your face?' Vivienne said, bluntly. It came across rude, but that wasn't her intention; she was just intrigued.

'I was at his house tonight and I told him that I wanted to end the relationship, and he turned so visibly angry and violent, I thought he was going to hit me . . . And he did. With the back of his right hand.' She swallowed sharply, and her voice began to tremble again. 'I didn't feel like going home, so I came here.' The bruise on her face was uncomfortable to look at. It was clear that a lot of rage and strength went into it.

'I'm sorry, I should have been there to support you.'

Amelie stood and refilled her glass of water. 'You couldn't have known. Plus, being mad at you wouldn't change anything. I got myself into this and I ignored my better judgment.'

'Don't beat yourself up.' Vivienne grabbed her hands that laid trembling in her lap.

'Could I stay here the night?'

There was no possible way she could say no, not after what Amelie had endured. It wouldn't have been fair. 'Of course you can. Go to my room and make yourself comfortable, I'm just going to finish up here.'

'Thanks, Viv.'

She covered her typewriter with its hard plastic shell and slipped into bed. Amelie was already asleep, exhausted. It was relief that they were back on speaking terms. However, the reason for Amelie's return was still ambiguous. Was she desperate and in need of comfort? Or had she actually forgiven Vivienne?

Bonnie's tail slid across Vivienne's face. She woke and turned to her side, expecting to see Amelie. Yet she wasn't there. Nor was she in the kitchen or lounge room. It was odd. Maybe she needed space to breathe and had left. After breakfast, Vivienne drove to Amelie's house to investigate. She rang the doorbell four times, but there was no answer. Both of them had a set of keys to each other's places, in case of an emergency. It wasn't clear what qualified as an emergency, but considering the events of the previous night, it was justifiable.

Vivienne called out. 'Amelie.' But there was no response. She ran up to her bedroom—the door was open, and clothes laid scattered around the room. When she opened the closet, only a few items of apparel filled the racks. Like Amelie's torn black leather jacket that she was too lazy to get tailored and her polka dot dress that she absolutely adored, until she didn't.

Her clothes were gone. Her car was gone. And she was gone.

CHAPTER TWELVE

'I would like to report a missing person.'

The police officer glanced up from his desk and stared at Vivienne, unimpressed. 'How can I help you today?' he said, lowering his glasses.

'I think my friend Amelie has been abducted. Or taken.'

'And what makes you say that?' The officer took his glasses off completely and raised his eyebrows, exposing a cluster of wrinkles on his forehead.

'When I went to her house this morning, her clothes were missing, and her room was in complete disarray.' The frantic explanation stormed through the soundless station.

'And when exactly did you see her last?'

Vivienne raised her hands up in front of herself and counted the hours on her fingers. 'About eleven hours ago.'

A ridiculing laugh left the officer's mouth. He must have thought she was crazy. 'Look, I don't appreciate people wasting my time. Maybe your friend has gone out for the day. Maybe she's with her family? Try that before causing a scene.' Calling Amelie's parents would have been the rational first step. But rationality had exited the building along with Amelie. Vivienne looked at the police officer and reluctantly thanked him. He looked like he wanted to kill himself, and so would she if she were stuck at that desk all day. A part of her sympathised with him. She walked out the station and a switch flicked in her brain. She had transformed into a hound set on finding Amelie. She stepped into her car and thought about what to do next. Was driving to Tours a crazy idea? Maybe Amelie had gone to be with her parents for a few days. Vivienne had nothing more important to do. Nothing more pressing than finding Amelie. She had a pit in her stomach. What if Jac had done something to her? What if his violent lust for her had made him do something terrible? Vivienne's mind was spinning. Even if Amelie wasn't there, Gabriel and Julia had a right to know about the distressing events of the previous night.

She grabbed her coat from the back seat and covered her head, then made a run for the front door.

She stood there, sopping wet, and knocked firmly. 'Have you seen Amelie?'

'Vivienne? Come in, you're soaked.' Julia said. 'What are you doing here?' She looked worried.

'All of Amelie's clothes were gone from her wardrobe and so was the car.' Julia took a woollen blanket from one of the top shelves in the kitchen and wrapped it around Vivienne.

A letter that had been carefully torn on the top laid on the table. It was the only thing on the table. 'Amelie left this by the front door a few hours ago. We didn't see her, but this explained the situation.' Julia took the note out of the envelope and slid it towards her. The note was brief, only a few lines. She skimmed over it, but it felt like a riddle, which was the last thing Vivienne wanted. She wanted clarity. The second line read, 'I'm heading south, you know where I'll be. I just need some space.' Vivienne didn't know what was south, but Julia looked at ease.

'So what? She ran away?'

'We know roughly where she is.'

'Why are you so unbothered by this?' Julia stared at her

apologetically. Clearly, she knew more than she was letting on.

'I understand you're upset, but Amelie has a history of this.' She put her hand on Vivienne's shoulder. 'When she was seventeen, she ran away for a few weeks. She gets overwhelmed. She doesn't know how to lay down roots. Nomadic, one might say.' It surprised Vivienne to hear this. Nomadic wasn't a word she would use to describe Amelie. Sure, she could be abrupt and free-spirited, but that was different. Her mother wasn't describing the Amelie she knew. Julia didn't see Amelie through the same rose-coloured glasses that Vivienne did.

'So, you're suggesting she'll only be gone for a few weeks?'

'I'm sorry, Vivienne, but I think this could be a—' She struggled to find the word. 'An indefinite move.' Julia walked to the kitchen, grabbed a tea towel, and started to wipe the spotless bench. 'We got a call from the bank, not long before you arrived, letting us know that she withdrew and transferred half of her savings into a new account.'

'And how much was that, exactly?'

'About 190,000 francs.' Her ears, in denial, perked. The number confirmed that Amelie would not be back for a long time. It was heartbreaking. Especially because her last memory of Amelie wasn't a pleasant one. She wanted things to go back to how they were, but now all that was left was the bitter aftertaste of something that was once so sweet. Reading the letter reminded her of the one Thomas had left her. A letter was such a cowardly way out. A way to tell someone something without having to see the sadness on their face. A way to hurt someone and be a continent away. Tears fell down her cheek. Her naïvety prayed that this was temporary, that she'd see Amelie's face again in class. But what was the point of raising her hopes just for them to come crumbling down? 'Also, the note was a bit vague. Do you know what, or who, may have caused her to run away?' Vivienne stood up from the table, brushed her damp coat, and prepared to leave. Julia sat still, waiting for a response.

'She had an altercation with her boyfriend last night.'

'What was his name?'

'Not sure last name, but his first name was Jac.'

She nodded to the information but didn't seem surprised. 'Amelie had told me she was seeing someone . . . Do you think he was the reason? Why she left?'

'I'm not sure why she left, but it's a possibility, for sure.' Jac was definitely a factor, but was he the sole reason? Vivienne didn't want to contemplate the reason, because if she did, she would somehow have found a way to blame herself. Amelie leaving was undeniable karma, a mutant cell that would eventually plague the rest of the body, a lesson from the universe not to take *who* or *what* she had for granted. Vivienne stayed with Julia long enough to get answers, but no matter how long she'd stay, she would never get closure.

She couldn't go back to her apartment. It was too overwhelming, being left alone with her own thoughts, knowing only hours earlier, Amelie was asleep in her bed. Nights like these reminded her of the value of Adrion. His arms could make her forget about anything.

'I'm going to be late. Again.' Vivienne opened one of the drawers that had been designated to her and pulled out a fresh pair of underwear and trousers. She hadn't moved in with Adrion, but they had decided it was more efficient to leave a few of the essentials at each other's places.

'Do you want me to drive you?'

'No, I have my car, remember,' she said, struggling to pull up her pants. On her way to the door, Sofia ran up to her and handed her a banana, then gave her a quick two-minute spiel on the importance of breakfast. Sofia was one of the kindest people she had ever met. Not to mention she was amusing, whether she intended to be or not.

Vivienne paced down the corridor, took two lefts, and arrived at the lecture hall. Her classes had been moved to a new room the previous term and it still confused her. Everyone was seated, but the class was devoid of life. It had lost its charm. It had lost Amelie. Vivienne awkwardly moved to the front of the room, looking for an appropriate place to sit. They had both started this journey together, but it seemed only one of them would end it.

Professor Clarke whispered Vivienne's name from her desk. She expected another firm reminder on punctuality. 'You're close with Amelie, correct?'

'Yes, I am.'

'I got notified today that she's transferred. Were you aware of this?'

This confirmed it; Amelie wasn't coming back. 'I am now.'

'It's quite sudden. I was only informed a couple of minutes before class. A shame, she was bright. No wonder you two got along.'

'Do you know where she's transferred to?'

'No clue, sorry. I just wanted to ask you to make sure I was getting the facts right. Alright, go sit, don't want to keep everyone waiting too long.' Professor Clarke brought the students' attention to herself and continued her lecture on famous female poets.

There was a component to life that craved simplicity, and hers had been lacking it. It may have been dull, but the mind and body needed maintenance. The past few days had been so convoluted, and she needed time to process. She walked to a nearby art supply store and purchased a medium-sized canvas, two paintbrushes, and some charcoal. There was something so beautiful about painting. It was a way for her to shut her mind off and give herself fully. A way to be vulnerable. Writing, as much as she loved it, didn't make her feel vulnerable. It made her feel empowered, but not vulnerable.

She also loved the serenity of museums. They were arguably one of humanity's greatest creations. The fact that humanity could collectively see the value of something that didn't have any true function. Art and culture were what separated humans from something bestial. She enjoyed uncovering the meaning behind an artist's work. Or making her own. Often, the art she found most appealing was from the most troubled artists. Vivienne could see their vulnerability through their art, which she found admirable. She perched her canvas against a tree and laid out the brushes and jagged piece of charcoal. She started to slash the canvas, budling up momentum until she was bruising it and leaving harsh dents. The harder she pressed, the more cathartic it felt. With every stroke and slash and stab came a sea of emotions. She rubbed some of the charcoal on her fingers and created what resembled a mouth, then a nose, then the eyes. She poured some water over her brush and faded the background, turning it pastel grey. She didn't know the person she had created. She didn't want to know or become this person. She took out the lighter from her pocket, struck it, turned the canvas on its side, and started to burn it. She stood there and watched it burn. So much for preserving art.

'We were expecting you for dinner.'

'Sorry, I lost track of time.'

'That's all good. You're here for dessert and that's what matters.' Sofia stood over the stove, tempering chocolate in a large glass bowl. 'Do you mind getting me the whisk? It's just in the cupboard below you.' Vivienne kneeled and scanned for it. 'Oh, it's right here. I would lose my head if it wasn't stuck on.' Sofia picked up the metal whisk and waved it around. 'Can you keep an eye on the chocolate while I take the eclairs out of the oven?'

'Sure.' A stream of smoke soared to the ceiling as the oven doors opened. Sofia picked up the tray with a tea towel and darted to place it on the kitchen bench. She uncontrollably tossed the dish as the heat burnt her, and a few of the eclairs ended up scattered on the floor. With a tissue, she picked them up, brushed them off, and placed them on the bench as if nothing had happened. Vivienne continued to passively stir the chocolate and watched as Sofia shuffled, disoriented, through the kitchen. It was like watching one of those animated cartoons she used to see on the television as a kid.

'Come help me pipe the cream into these,' Sofia said after finally composing herself. Vivienne stood next to her as she demonstrated how to pipe the eclairs. It seemed easy enough, so she didn't pay too close attention, but that was far from the case. The cream started to bulge out of every crevice and the piping bag even burst at one stage. Sofia couldn't contain her laughter at the failed attempts. Between those that were unsuccessfully piped, and the ones that had dropped on the floor, they only had eight good eclairs. Adrion appeared from his room as they doused the tops of the eclairs in chocolate. He didn't say anything; he just stood and admired as Vivienne and Sofia talked and plated the eclairs.

'Adrion.' It had taken her a few seconds to notice him.

'Look who the cat dragged in.' He pulled the hair away from her face and pecked her forehead. 'These look fantastic.' He snatched one of the eclairs and jumped backwards. Sofia picked up the wooden spoon and chased him in circles around the kitchen, repeating a phrase in Italian. Vivienne couldn't understand what she was saying, but this looked well-rehearsed. On the other hand, Adrion was prancing around the room with a grin wider than a ravine.

'You mongrel,' she yelled. It was pointless chasing him. He was too fast. 'Well, since Adrion has no manners, we might as well dig in.' They all reached for an eclair and shoved it in their mouths. If Vivienne hadn't been part of the production process, she would've thought they were from a bakery, they tasted that good.

'You two go off, I'll clean up.'

'Thanks, Mum.'

There wasn't much good to be found recently, but when she looked hard enough, it was still there. Vivienne explained what had happened to Amelie. He had only met her a few times, but he liked her—and he practically knew her on a personal level from how much Vivienne had talked about her. It felt nice to alleviate the weight on her shoulders. It was surprisingly even more cathartic than stabbing charcoal at a canvas for three hours.

'You and my mum were made for each other.' Adrion slipped the sentence into the conversation.

The comment was random, but he wasn't wrong. 'Love Sofia.'

'Not as much as me, I hope.' Vivienne giggled. The joke wasn't funny, but his unintentionally serious tone made it unbearable not to laugh.

'No, Adrion, you don't have to worry.' Vivienne took a large breath to stop the laughing.

'Good. I want you all to myself.' They both laid on their backs, staring at the ceiling. There was a serene silence. 'Do you—want to move in?'

Vivienne frowned. The question caught her off guard. How could she answer something so forward? Moving in with someone sounded awful. She loved Adrion. When she took her clothes off, she still didn't feel close enough to him. She wanted him to be inside her, but not constantly. She was still a person. A person who loved her privacy and comfort equally as much. She couldn't give that up, not for anyone. Without a moment to process, her mouth opened, and the words bolted forward.

'Why would I want to move in?'

CHAPTER THIRTEEN

Vivienne walked towards Hugo's office. Pierre, the illustrator, gave her an unnerving look. 'I bought you a ham, pickle, and mustard sandwich, but they didn't have any—' Her train of thought was suddenly interrupted as she rushed into the office. In the chairs across from Hugo were two men in black suits, both bald with beards. One of the men spun their head around and stared at Vivienne. Hugo took the pen that he had resting between his lips and signed a sheet of paper encased in a black folder, then handed it to the man on the right of him. 'Sorry, Vivienne, we'll just be a moment.'

'Actually, we have all we need. Thank you for your time and we will be in contact shortly.' Both of the men stood up and took turns shaking Hugo's hand, then left the room. Hugo rubbed his eyes and leaned back into his chair, looking at the ceiling. His face was riddled with defeat. It was as if he had been sentenced to death. In some ways, he had.

'Who were they?' Vivienne pulled out a chair and sat.

'Lawyers, from Reed's.' It became evident to her what was happening, but she was confident Hugo wasn't going to cave.

'How much did they offer?' she said, blatantly, without dancing around the question.

'I can't disclose the amount . . . But a lot. Probably triple what this joint's worth.'

'You're going to take it. Aren't you?' Her tone was no longer poised.

'Yes.'

'That easily.'

'Vivienne, I have mouths to feed. Sitting around on our arses doesn't pay my mortgage. They were doing me a favour. I could've waited for them to completely destroy us but what would've been the point of that? Deep down, you know that.' Hugo was right; there was no possible way they could have competed with Reed's. However, she didn't think he would go down without a fight. She envisaged him as a gladiator of the industry, not a wimp.

'And what about everyone else? You think we don't have mouths to feed?'

'I'm not going to have this argument with you. Unless you can find the money to keep us afloat, I don't see a solution. I love this place, but not enough to go bankrupt.' His voice started to raise. Guilt was more prevalent on his face now, like a soldier who had abandoned his post in the spirit of self-preservation. Vivienne arguing was making his decision even more unbearable. She could fix this.

'Fine. *I'll* find the money.' She slammed the door behind her. Every head in the office darted up. She walked to her car outside, placed both her hands on the window, and leaned forward.

'Think,' she closed her eyes and muttered to herself. Where could she find the sort of money the company needed? Her parents definitely couldn't have helped—their finances were all over the place. Would banks loan to broke university students? Maybe she could reason with Reed's and somehow persuade them to leave their clients alone. It was a ridiculous idea, but she had nothing to lose in trying.

The Reed's building was nice, modern. It had the type of glass entry that went around in circles, which she always found fascinating as a kid.

'I would like to speak with the person in charge.' The receptionist behind the desk glanced up from the bulky computer and squinted her eyes. Vivienne's office didn't have a computer. She had used one once at the university library, but she didn't like the feel of the keys.

'Do you have an appointment today?' Vivienne could tell the receptionist knew she didn't have an appointment.

'No. I don't.'

'Well, I can't let you see him.'

'Just please, it's urgent.' The woman stood up from her desk and disappeared down the corridor for a few seconds. When she reappeared, a man was next to her.

'What can I help you with today, dear?' the man asked, in a thick American accent.

'I'm here to talk about—I need to talk—' A stuttered attempt to speak escaped Vivienne's mouth. She planned to confront Reed's, but she hadn't devised anything further than that.

'Alright, how about you come into my office and we can talk? Can you do that for me?' Why was he speaking to her like that? Like she was stupid. She utterly despised people who were condescending towards her. Just because this man wore a suit and tie didn't mean he was in any way smarter or more intelligent than her. Vivienne politely nodded at him. Maybe if she came off meek and helpless, she could earn sympathy. She needed to save Hugo from himself. If she didn't, she knew he would live out the rest of his days filled with regret. That couldn't be allowed—the company was his pride and joy.

The man ushered her into his office, which was beautifully designed and decorated. Bookshelves lined either wall. There was a large globe in the far-left corner which also doubled as a liquor cabinet. It was more glamorous than any of the offices at Hugo's firm, which were mainly furnished with filing cabinets and the occasional desk lamp.

'Here, take a seat,' the man said, pouring himself a generous glass of liquor. 'Would you like one?' Vivienne waved her hand with disapproval. She had alcohol at home. She wasn't there to have a drink and polite chat—she was there to get answers. 'What can I do for you? You seemed a bit panicked earlier. Also, the name's Samuel.' He reached over, ready to shake her hand.

'Vivienne.'

'Well, Vivienne, what can I help you with?' Samuel sniffed his drink and took a big gulp, maintaining an uncomfortable amount of eye contact the entire time.

'I work for a publishing firm not far from here, and your company, *Reed's*, is trying to buy us out.'

'So, what, you're looking for a job?'

A sharp exhale left her nose and attacked the insulting comment. 'No, I'm not looking for a job. I'm asking you to stop expanding your business. Don't you have enough? Do you realise that you are running publishing companies who have been around for decades to the ground? All you people care about is making more money. You don't care about the authenticity or effort that goes into publishing something.' Her rant was less concise than she intended, but everything was true; Reed's was destroying the industry.

'I hear what you're saying, but I'm just a manager, I can't help. It doesn't affect me in the slightest whether Reed's expands. But if you try to fight this, it'll be an uphill battle.' Samuel stood up and walked around the room. 'Why do you think I'm in this industry? It's because I understand the value of books. The world's changing, unfortunately. And you're right, the people above me do only care about money. I just try to make a difference where I can.' Vivienne was slightly shocked that Samuel sympathised with her. Her initial impression of him may have been wrong. 'I know I can't help, but I really admire your devotion. If you are ever in need of a job, I might be able to pull some strings on my end.' He took one of the business cards from his desk and handed it to her. She appreciated the gesture. However, she would never have taken the opportunity. She respected Hugo too much. It was naïve to think that confronting Reed's would have resolved anything. There must have been another way, but it was eluding her.

The cables of a television were required to connect perfectly. If one wire crossed incorrectly, no sound could be heard. If a cable broke, the picture projected may distort, or even disappear. Human relationships were like a television. When a person was born, they had all their wires intact. A shiny new screen, unscathed. But slowly, those wires became damaged, taken, and tangled. The screen distorted. The wires of a television could be contorted, but they could also be refurbished and fixed. A technician, perhaps? But it could be hard to find a good technician. Word of mouth certainly wasn't a reliable source. Several bad technicians could leave a television unusable. However, an excellent one could not only return it to its original state but enhance it. Sometimes, the best technicians weren't even the most renowned. Sometimes, they were apprentices. Despite this, a television was not expected to last forever. Nothing lasted forever, so what made love the exception? Some people threw their television away once it ceased to work. Some clung onto it, too scared to invest in a new one. Love was somewhat like a television.

Vivienne had been unintentionally senseless, and Adrion had gone into hibernation. All calls had gone to voicemail. What Vivienne had said was wrong and she could see that now, clearly. Sometimes, she forgot to choose her words carefully, and her mouth and her brain became one. Adrion was like a wrecking ball that slammed in without an eviction notice. He knew the duress that she had been under recently. Why would he ask her to move in with him? Why did he think placing that on her was a good idea? Panic set in, and she had reacted accordingly. In her mind, the comment was insignificant, but she could hear Adrion's heart skip a beat when she said it. She simultaneously wanted him to forgive her and was upset that he had misinterpreted what she meant. Every time he didn't pick up the phone, she imagined him on the other side of the line, listening to her ramble. Adrion had most certainty heard the messages she had left. He would come around eventually—he had to.

Pen was not on paper. Vivienne placed the blue metal pen onto the frayed notebook that had worn from the vigorous hand movements. She flicked through, hopeful for inspiration. Nothing came. The ideas for her novel had been steadily coming to her, although she had been too distracted to write anything solid and meaningful. Vivienne retrieved a different notebook from her bookshelf, one that was new, then unevenly tore out a page. There must have been a way to save the company, she just wasn't thinking hard enough. An hour passed. Then another, and again, nothing. And then it hit her. Vivienne could ask Amelie's parents for the money and pitch it as a business investment. It may have been inconsiderate under the circumstances, but Vivienne was prepared to leave her dignity behind for a greater cause. She was sure Hugo would be open to negotiating something along those terms. Besides, Julia didn't seem that bothered by Amelie leaving. Vivienne didn't like begging for money—or trying to justify it—but she was desperate. Amelie would understand. Vivienne stared blankly outside her window, tapping her pen on the notebook. In the morning, she would drive up to Tours for the second time that week, convince Julia and Gabriel to help the company, and then her life could resume. It felt almost too easy to be true.

Her life had become so fast paced, only when things finally slowed did she realise that. Occasionally, she imagined joining some random commune that just picked berries and laid in the sun. Sounded nice, but she'd get bored. Plus, who would take Marion to her appointments? And who would take the role of Hugo's personal errand girl? Who would feed Bonnie? Who'd love Adrion? Maybe she didn't want to completely abandon her life, but she longed for things to slow down. It wasn't only her life that was fast paced. The whole world had become fast paced. Everything had become about constantly consuming—even she was a part of the cycle, with her expensive clothes and her love for finer things. She thought that Hugo and the company would be immune, but nothing was immune to this vicious progression. People and businesses came and tried to monopolise everything. However, the fact that they were coming for publishing firms and bookshops was unacceptable. Publishing a book was about more than money. It was about creating something beautiful, creating a legacy that would stand the test of time. Vivienne believed books were more valuable than most people. All that Reed's—and other corporations like it—cared about was what would fly off the shelves fastest and how they could line their pockets as quickly as possible. Books, texts, painting, music, art had all started to feel ingenuine. A shell of its once authentic self. Those hidden gems started to become rarer and rarer. But if she could help Hugo, it was her way of preserving the culture. Not many people understood the importance of these things. Then again, not many of them had grown up in a bookshop where books replaced walls.

'Vivienne, you're back again,' Julia said, confused and almost suspicious. Turning up unannounced was beginning to turn into a common occurrence. She would simply call, but she didn't have their number, and she had learned to love the drive.

'Yes. I know this is highly unusual, but could I come in and talk to you about something?' Vivienne said with subtle urgency.

'Of course, our doors are always open.' Julia led her into the gorgeous living room. The fireplace was on with fresh logs laid on top. It wasn't cold, so it must have been purely for decoration. Outside, Gabriel was pruning the dense, overgrown hedges. Vivienne found it odd that they hadn't simply hired someone to do it. 'What can I help you with?' Julia sat down.

'You know the company I work for, the small publishing firm?'

'Yes, I remember. Did you get that promotion you mentioned a while back?'

'No, still junior editor, but I prefer it that way,' Vivienne responded. 'But the reason I'm here is that the company is having some issues.'

'What type of issues?'

'Do you know the publishing company Reed's?'

Julia nodded. 'Yes, I've heard of them. Actually recently bought a few books that were published by them.'

'Well, they're a big US company and, as you can imagine, terrible news for us. And we're struggling.' She sighed. It still didn't sit right with her, asking for money. She hated taking from people. No matter their generosity, she always felt indebted to them, and she never wanted to feel that way.

'Would a charitable donation help?' Vivienne's face eased. She didn't have to even ask; Julia was offering. Instantly, the guilt she felt was alleviated.

'That's what I wanted to talk about. Hugo and I wouldn't take handouts, him especially. He's too proud. However, if you became investors or silent partners of some kind, maybe that could work. He's thinking of selling but I know it would be a mistake. It would ultimately ruin him.' Julia thought about the idea for a second. She and Gabriel had an unimaginable amount of wealth. The exact amount was unknown to her, but she was sure that this 'investment' would have little to no effect on them.

'It could work. I would have to run it past Gabriel, but I don't see why he would be opposed. Especially since it's in good faith.' Julia was a hero in her eyes. She had the means *and* wanted to help, which was rare, like finding truffles in dirt. 'Quick question, though. You mentioned Hugo was thinking of selling. It hasn't preceded past that, though, right?'

'Not entirely.' Vivienne paused and thought. 'There were some lawyers from Reed's and Hugo signed something in a black folder or document. Not too sure.'

Julia's face switched to uncertainty. 'Did he specify to you what he signed?'

'No, sorry.'

'Vivienne, I'm willing to help, but my suspicions tell me that Hugo may have already made up his mind. Find out what he's signed, and we can discuss further,' she said with a sorry look.

'Do you mean to tell me he's already signed it away?'

'Well, don't you think it's odd that Reed's lawyers were there as he signed something?'

'I don't know. I just thought that he was expressing his interest.' Vivienne's mouth drooped. In her haste to save the company, she didn't stop to question whether there was still anything left to save. The pleasant feeling of success disintegrated in her hands. 'Can't we just get it waived? It's only been a day.'

'It's a possibility, but the chances are unlikely. Reed's wouldn't comply and would most likely refuse. That would mean if we wanted to get it waived, we would have to fight some form of legal battle. Even if you challenged it and tried to get it overturned, it would take months. It simply wouldn't be worth it.' Julia paused. 'We could set up a mediation with someone in

Reed's and try and talk them out of what Hugo signed.' This all sounded too complicated to Vivienne, and Hugo would definitely not have agreed to something like that. Everything said was speculation, but it added up. He had signed the deed over to Reed's and now there was nothing to be done. She couldn't save Amelie and she couldn't save the company. She had failed, her efforts in vain. 'I'm sorry, Vivienne.'

'Sorry' was nice, but it wouldn't change anything.

'Also, I don't know if this is a good time to bring this up, but it just came to mind, and I thought you have a right to know. We recently hired a PI to investigate this Jac you told us about. Apparently, he had two dropped assault charges and a restraining order, issued by his previous girlfriend.' Vivienne didn't know how to take it. The lines between good and bad news had been erased and greyed out. At least this was some form of closure. And at least she was right, Jac was bad news.

'I wish I knew. I wish I could have done something, Julia.'

'No, this was not your battle to fight. You have enough going on in your life. My sympathies for your mother's cancer, and may she recover.' Vivienne appreciated the comfort yet was offended that Amelie had talked about her mother's condition. It wasn't her information to tell. There was no benefit in getting upset, though. Everyone had been through enough, and Julia was on her side, she couldn't forget.

'Thank you.'

'You've had a long drive. You're welcome to stay here the night. The guest bedroom is made up.' Vivienne had already attempted doing a round trip to Tours. It was a six-hour drive that was hard on the legs. And an opportunity to sleep in silk sheets was not one she could pass up.

Before Vivienne went to bed, she strolled through the vineyard, which this time was full of grapes ready to be harvested.

The moon shone above her, another thing yet again out of reach, tantalising her.

Vivienne stepped out of her car and paced towards the building. As she opened the mint-green door, she got a glimpse of Hugo, who was bringing out cardboard boxes from his office. When she opened the door wider, she was shocked. All the desks had been stripped clean with the exception of one—hers. Hugo noticed Vivienne and gave her a smile filled with sadness. He appeared reminiscent, like a person who had over-analysed an old picture of themselves and wondered how they got to where they were. The company was who he was. A significant portion of his identity, and his legacy.

Vivienne crept closer to him. 'Hi.'

'Hey.'

'I'll start packing my stuff.'

'Thank you.' As the room emptied, the atmosphere became colder. There was no more furniture, no more memories or clients to insulate the rooms that were now bare. It was quiet between them. They hadn't exactly ended their last conversation on positive terms.

'You're right.' Hugo sighed, as he brought out the last box from his office. Vivienne glanced up from the desk drawer she was emptying. 'I should have fought.' He chuckled with a slight tear in his eye. 'You know, my father built this company from the ground up. He watched the construction progress every day until it was complete. He was so proud to have something that he could call his own . . . I'm just glad he's dead.' The tear that had built up in his left eye finally rolled down his face. 'This would have crushed his soul,' he said, wiping it away. Vivienne stood up, retrieved the car keys from her pocket, and pushed them towards him.

'Thank you for taking a chance on me,' she said softly.

He placed his hands on hers and pushed back. 'Keep the car,

as a parting gift. I have no use for it, and you deserve it.'

'I shouldn't.' She wanted to keep the car. Buying a new one was not in her budget. But Hugo was in a fragile state, and she didn't want to take advantage of it.

'Please, it is the least I can do.' He always treated her well, with dignity and respect. He treated her as a person, not a resource. And not just her, but all his employees. Some of them had been at the company for almost a decade. They, undoubtably, would have been hit heavily by the abrupt ending. The ending to an era. She slid the keys into her bag and nodded at him.

'Take care of yourself.'

'You too,' she replied.

'Lock the door on your way out.' Hugo turned his back and walked out the door. The door that was no longer his, but Reed's.

Vivienne finished shortly after Hugo left. She carried the box with her possessions and placed it in the boot of her car. The thought that the company was gone hadn't quite hit her. A part of her was in denial, hoping that she would turn up the next day, ready to meet a new client or help Hugo run errands. Or even see Pierre, during lunch break, drop the sauce from his sandwich all over himself. At least she could focus on her writing. She had fewer excuses now.

Vivienne hauled the box up to her apartment, blindly stepping up the stairs. As she approached, she could see a pair of feet standing by the front door. The face wasn't visible due to the angle and position of the box. However, with every step, the figure became clearer. 'What's with the box?' Adrion said, standing stiff on the floor mat. It was uncertain how long he had been standing there waiting for her, but she presumed a while.

'The company was taken over.'

'Shit, I'm sorry.' The box made a thump as it hit the ground. Vivienne cracked her back and looked at him briefly in the eye, unable to maintain contact. It felt wrong. Only now, she realised how cruel she had been. Regardless of the pressure pounding her, she had disregarded his feelings. Yet he was the one standing at her door, waiting. Their positions should have been reversed.

'Nothing can be done, I guess.' The awkwardness trickled from her mouth. Adrion faced the ground. She had taken the wind from his usually confident sail. Vivienne was clueless how to repair the situation. Where was she supposed to begin? Instead, she opened her mouth, hoping the words would find her.

'I don't think I've told you this, but it was the first history lecture I ever attended at the university, and you were there. I was three rows behind you and Monsieur Belan called your name. You only said a few words, but my stomach churned. Something came over me. This dissociative feeling, or something. Still that feeling passes through me when I see you.' She stepped closer towards him. 'I don't articulate what I want to say very well sometimes, which I know is ironic as all I do is read and write, but I'm trying.' Her voice quietened and tone softened. 'Sometimes, I just don't feel worthy of your love... Without you, I'm a little bit empty, and it scares me that you have this hold over me. If I move in with you, I'm scared I might lose you. I don't want to go too fast and end up derailed. I've lost too much lately to lose you.' Vivienne paused momentarily. 'What I said was stupid and I hope that we can—' Before she could finish her sentence, Adrion grabbed the back of her waist and drew her close to him. A dark shadow casted upon Vivienne's face as he leaned in and kissed her.

His lips drew inches from hers, their noses still virtually touching. 'Vivienne, you can be impulsive, and bad-mannered, and yes, at times, just completely reckless. But I love you enough to see beyond that. I know you think I didn't notice you back then, but I did. I saw the way you would come into the class late, disorganised, and disorderly. You've had my attention much longer than when you called me that night at Amelie's. You're a complex person, there is no denying that, but that's what I fell in love with. I feel alive with you, whatever that entails.' He lifted his head away. 'You're going to have to try a lot harder to get rid of me,' he said in his rich, arcane voice. 'Now, let's go inside, I'm starving.' The joke eased the intensity. The unexpected intimate moment left her speechless. When they entered the apartment, Adrion flicked through the vinyls as he usually did. This was normal, this was right. *Together,* they were right.

CHAPTER FOURTEEN

Vivienne woke to Adrion's face in front of her. She uncovered herself carefully, insuring she did not interrupt his sleep.

Adrion tugged on her arm lightly without opening his eyes. 'No, stay in bed.' His raspy voice sauntered on her skin, the offer tempting her. The bed was warm, and Adrion's hair smelt musky. She looked at the bridge of his nose and the scar on his chin that was more obvious under the luminescent sunlight. He was so enticing, but she couldn't. Other plans awaited her. Less enjoyable plans.

'I can't. I have to go.'

'Okay. Don't be too long, though.'

'I won't.' She kissed him on the forehead and allowed him to plunge back into his slumber. Adrion was a vivid dreamer, much like herself. The only difference was that he sleepwalked and had ever since he was a child. Every so often, when he stayed the night, she would hear clattering around the apartment. The first time it happened, she thought someone was robbing her or had broken in. Instead, it was Adrion, who had left the bedroom and was wandering around aimlessly. Vivienne dressed herself quietly and made breakfast, which consisted of a few small carrots and dip. Marion had a consultation with Dr Dupont that had been rescheduled to an earlier date. Which was wasn't an inconvenience except for the seven o'clock wakeup. Marion was now too weak to drive from all the chemo that had been relentlessly pumped through her veins. Vivienne knew it was supposed to help, but some days, it was unbearable to watch the life slowly drain from her. The chemotherapy was supposedly curing her, but in the process, it had destroyed something else. Marion couldn't win. However, the chemotherapy was the lesser of the two evils.

When Vivienne arrived, Marion was sitting ready at the kitchen table. She was wearing a navy-blue V-neck top which was paired with beige pants and a pair of silver earrings that dangled and swayed with any minor movement. Vivienne thought she looked beautiful but refrained from saying anything. She had learned her lesson from the previous time she'd made a comment on how nice her mother's appearance was.

'What do you expect me to wear? A hospital gown? I have cancer, not brain damage. I know how to dress myself.' Vivienne didn't mean to insult her mother in any way, she just wanted to acknowledge that she looked nice. The comments were uncalled for, but she knew that if her mother's wit was intact, her condition must have been improving—or at least wasn't getting worse—which was something Vivienne was grateful for rather than upset about. Her father was standing, passively stirring his coffee, as he read the newspaper. Vivienne called his name, and he snapped out of his trance, then came up to her and hugged her with his free arm. Marion looked at Vivienne eagerly. She hated being late for their appointments. The hospital was only a short drive from their house—that, however, did not compensate for the long wait on arrival at the office. Although they had a specific time booked, it would typically take upwards of twenty minutes before they were invited into Doctor Dupont's office. Except this time, there was no wait. Instead, it looked as though he was waiting for them.

'Come in,' Dr Dupont said. He placed his hand gently on Marion's shoulder and led her into the office, Vivienne following shortly behind.

Dr Dupont took off his glasses, revealing a grim look that plagued his face. A face that had undoubtably been made so often that the wrinkles and fine lines of his face had adapted to that position. He was only in his early fifties, but his work had aged him at least fifteen years. 'The reason I moved this appointment up is that I have some difficult news to tell you. I reviewed the scans that you took last week, and we found something.' Vivienne placed her hand over her mouth nervously and leaned forward in her chair. 'You have developed metastatic cancer. The cancer spread. To your lower bowel and possibly other areas.' Marion stared at Dr Dupont with a blank expression and her hands placed over her purse in her lap. Vivienne looked at her mother, awaiting a reaction, but it was like looking at a statue.

'But you have a treatment, right? You can fix it?' Vivienne said, the words running out of her mouth with a tinge of panic.

'We have two options from here. Continue with chemo or try a surgical approach that is more—more radical. That would then be followed with more chemo.'

'And how long would I have if I left it untreated and went off chemo?' Marion replied. Behind her eyes, she was scared. Vivienne stared at her mother, terrified at the thought that surrendering to this disease was a viable option.

'Three to four months. Tops.'

'And what if we do the surgery and continue with the chemotherapy? What about then?' Vivienne raised her voice, which had filled to the brim with desperation.

'If we continue chemo without the surgery . . . twenty percent chance of full remission. With surgery, possibly sixty. But I do have to disclaim that the surgery comes with a lot of added risks. There is some chance you would not make it off the operating table.' This felt like a death sentence. The body that was supposed to keep her alive was killing her from the inside out. Marion had done everything. She had played by the rules. She had taken her medication, took the treatments, underwent every surgery. She had let them deconstruct her and reconstruct her over and over again. Vivienne knew she wouldn't go willingly, but she was scared that her mother wouldn't make it out the other side. She was so fragile now and her body was nowhere near as strong as her will. The army of cancer was consuming her.

'I'll do the surgery.' The idea loitered. Vivienne couldn't comprehend what her mother was saying. It was as if her ability to understand words had vanished.

'No. Mama, are you not listening? If you do this surgery, you could die. They are going to cut and prod you until there is nothing left and you are just a pile of flesh—' Vivienne's face wilted and she yelped. 'And then I'm not going to have a mother.' The words barely came out.

'This isn't living, Vivienne. I want to see the ocean.' Marion's voice shuddered, her strong, composed façade torn down.

Vivienne collected herself and faced away from her mother to look at Dr Dupont. 'When would the surgery take place?'

'Three or four days. We want to go in as soon as possible.' It felt like there was someone inside her tugging and clawing on the walls of her chest.

'No. It's too soon.'

'Vivienne, I don't have a choice, please, my baby. Please, please, I can't do this if I have to watch you cry.' Marion stroked Vivienne's head and turned her face away to conceal her agony.

'No, Mama. You can't.' The paper tissues in Vivienne's hand had disintegrated from the tears. Doctor Dupont stood there, useless.

'Vivienne, don't be naïve, for God's sake. I am dying. Without this surgery, I am going to die. With this surgery, I still might die. But I haven't fought this hard just to give up. I fought endlessly to bring you into this world, and I will fight endlessly to keep me here.' The sentence pierced through Vivienne's body. She grabbed her stomach as if to check whether she was actually wounded. In that moment, something clicked within her brain. Suddenly, her frantic look started to dissipate, her eyes began to dry, and all that was left to remind her of her bestial anguish were her red, puffy eyes. There was something comforting about Marion's words. She brought life into the world; surely, she could also ground it, sew it, and stitch it down.

'Okay,' Vivienne said, sponging her last tears with the corner of her sleeve.

Not a single one of them spoke. Dr Dupont was rattled by what had unfolded before him. He had certainly handed death to several people, but it appeared that he had never managed to truly grapple with it. Vivienne had to remind herself that he was human too. It was difficult to admit, but she viewed medical professionals as robots who had muted feelings. This perception was based on the few interactions she'd had with them. Through her recent exposure, she realised they did in fact have feelings, and she felt a sense of guilt for categorising them unfairly.

It always remained a mystery to her whether or not executioners felt anything when they killed someone. How did they go home at the end of a day with blood on their hands? Yes, the people they killed may have been bad—or, more fittingly, evil—but how could they live with themselves? Who provided them with the jurisdiction to take a life? Were they any better than the killers? Could killing be justified? Vivienne was sure that the people who were on death row could justify their actions. Again, the line between good and bad was grey. The death penalty had been outlawed a few years prior, but she still thought about the question sometimes. When they arrived home from the hospital, everything felt bleak. Marion made their house a home, and without her, there was no home. Louis was crushed by the news, yet he remained stoic and strong for Marion, which was vital, as Vivienne had shut down and couldn't have been much support. She hugged her mother for a while. Louis came and wrapped his arms around them both, creating an unbreakable sphere. They were unaware at the time, but this moment would never occur again. Vivienne left soon after, away in her black Volkswagen that had recently become a getaway vehicle rather than a car.

The savoury scent danced through the apartment. Adrion was hunched over the stove, carefully guiding diced veal off the chopping board and into a pot. Vivienne dropped her bag at the door and walked towards him.

'Hey, you're back. Come here, try this, tell me if it's good,' Adrion said, cheerfully. Vivienne grabbed the spoon and placed it into the stew, skimming a gentle layer from the top.

'Oh, that's nice,' she replied. She would have added more salt, but she didn't want to ruin his rhythm. Watching him cook reminded her of how gentle and delicate he could be.

'You were off pretty early this morning.'

'I had to take Marion to the hospital.' Vivienne placed her hands on the kitchen bench and hauled herself up, facing directly towards Adrion, who was still focused on preparing the meal.

'And how is she? You should take me to see her soon.'

'Actually, the cancer has grown worse. She's having an operation in a few days.' Everything about her in that moment was automated and mechanical. Her countenance didn't change, nor did her tone. She had become so desensitised to Marion's condition over the course of the day that she was completely numb. Her mother's potential death had now become casual conversation.

'I'm sorry.' He sighed. 'It pains me that there is nothing I can do to help. If you want me there during the procedure, you know I'd be there with you.' Vivienne moved closer to Adrion, who was still stirring the stew, then took his left hand and caressed his fingers. The chances of her father turning up to the hospital for the surgery were slim. Louis had always been like that. Not cowardly, however lacking the strength to see his loved ones' suffering. Mainly Marion and herself, as they were the only family he had. Or, more appropriately, the only people he considered family. Maybe he shied away from those who were wounded around him because it reminded him too much of his own suffering as a child. Vivienne had read about it, how important the developmental stages of an adolescent were. All the experiences that one endured as a child would create the very fabric for who they became. That's why she believed Louis was the way he was. Adrion wasn't an alternative, or a replacement, but since her father was unlikely to be there for them, she needed another lifeline.

'Thank you,' Vivienne said with a mellow smile. 'And thank you for this delicious meal.' She kissed him on the cheek and hopped off the counter.

'We have a lecture tomorrow. Should we drive in together? That way, I can finally wake up to you before you manage to scurry away,' he joked.

'I can't. I have to swing past Professor Clarke's office and discuss a few things. But let's catch coffee after we listen to Monsieur Belan's bullshit for two hours.' Whenever Vivienne made a nasty comment about their history teacher, Adrion would roll his eyes with disapproval. He was adored by Monsieur Belan. Some would say it was because he was a bright student. Vivienne would have argued that Adrion was leaning towards being a teacher's pet. If it were up to her, she would have never taken history, just literature. But she was required to take two subjects, and history by far was the most tolerable.

'I don't know why you hate him.'

'Well, firstly, his views are outdated.' By 'outdated', what she truly meant was that he was a misogynistic prick. No one had picked up on his subtle disdain towards women, but she had. Whenever he talked about women, he would act like they were inferior. Vivienne could sense undertones of a messy divorce. Adrion was too oblivious to realise. Vivienne strongly believed that the university should have already sacked him. He—and his ideologies—were far past their expiration date. 'And secondly, he looks odd.'

'You can't just dislike someone because they "look odd".'

'Watch me.'

The morning approached, and again, she was leaving Adrion early to attend to other matters. She looked down at him from above, curled up with a pillow in his arms. He was a gracious sleeper, she had to give him that.

The university had undergone renovations in the previous term, and all the lecture rooms had been relocated, and so had Professor Clarke's office. Which confused her as the university was a glorified maze. However, with some dumb luck, she found it, along with the professor, who was halfway between standing and sitting on her desk, quietly reading. Vivienne peeped through the window and knocked on the door.

The professor signalled for her to come in. 'Vivienne, you're here early. How can I help?'

'I just came to let you know that I might be unable to attend some of your lectures over the next few weeks.' Professor Clarke laid her book down, spine side up, and gave Vivienne her undivided attention.

'How come?'

'I have some family issues that need my attention... My mother has cancer.' As soon as she spoke, she felt as if she had crossed a line. Professor Clarke wasn't there for her to dump her trauma on, she was there to teach literature.

'I'm sorry to hear that. Recently diagnosed or has this been ongoing?' The mood shifted. Vivienne was caught off guard by the question. Was Professor Clarke also crossing a line? She didn't know a whole heap about professional conduct, but asking students personal questions didn't seem proper. Yet Professor Clarke didn't fit easily into the normal professional categories. She was different. She recognised and treated Vivienne as an equal.

'It's been ongoing for a while now, although she has taken a turn for the worse recently.' A dismal look appeared on the professor's face, as if Vivienne had unleashed something kept hidden.

'My mother passed from what the doctors presumed was cancer. Not my biological mother, if that's important, but my mother nonetheless.' She took the glasses that rested on her head and placed them next to the book. 'I was probably just younger than you. I regret not spending more time with her in the months leading up to her death. She passed within weeks of discovering it. Everywhere, like a plague.' Vivienne was confused, unable to process what she was telling her. Was Suzan Clarke adopted? Also, the question remained, why was she telling her this? 'Well, I won't keep you. Thank you for letting me know, and I'm here if you need.' She rested her hand gently on Vivienne's shoulder. 'I understand how difficult this can be. I hope she makes a recovery.'

'Thank you, Professor.'

Her interest and subtle infatuation with Professor Clarke had risen even more. She always looked up to her achievements, using them as a sort of professional standard she one day hoped to meet, but now she was intrigued about her past. The past that created such a refined woman.

Vivienne dragged herself to Monsieur Belan's lecture, which destroyed every ounce of inspiration she had. She hoped he would suddenly fall to the ground of a heart attack during one of his lectures. He was the short straw, but she couldn't overlook the fact that she also drew a long, broad straw: Professor Clarke.

CHAPTER FIFTEEN

Vivienne and Adrion sat in front of Marion. A nurse paced down the corridor and entered the room, simultaneously wrenching the curtain to one side and handing Marion a clip board with some papers attached.

'Could you please double check that the information is correct and sign at the bottom? The anaesthetist will be in shortly to discuss a few things.' The nurse wrapped a slim, plastic wrist band around Marion. 'Other than that, you are all set . . . You're in good hands.' She moved back and gave them a toothless smile, then pulled the light-blue curtain behind her. Vivienne watched as her mother unfolded her glasses and squinted at the sheets of paper. Marion had been through this relentless process before, over the course of several painstaking months. All that the papers required were the individual's identification and full consent to the procedure. Basically, everything that would cover their arse. Their way of shifting the blame onto a higher power—a way of creating a blameless death. If Marion died that day, it wasn't the incompetence of the doctors, it was the fault of the cancer. Right? Vivienne tried to initiate conversation with her mother, but the atmosphere was too merciless. Neither of them were actually there, both imagining white sand slipping through their feet, a simpler time.

Adrion was grim in his seat, but it was only fitting. Anything that affected her would ultimately affect him. If Marion's grip weakened and she fell from this physical place, he would very likely be left to pick up the pieces.

The three of them sat and watched as the sun slowly descended in front of them through two rectangular windows—that were left ajar—opposite the bed. Marion closed her eyes and allowed for the sunlight to hit her face. She was peaceful, lying there. It may not have been the beach, but it was a pleasant spectacle. A frame of a life beyond hospital gowns and intravenous drips. Vivienne was conscious of every one of Marion's movements. She looked at her mother almost every day and yet there were still things that she hadn't noticed. How her baby hairs swayed with any minor movement in the air.

The anaesthetist visited just as the last glimmer of light vanished. He spoke, but no one listened. Just more words with little meaning. Minutes after he left, two orderlies came and unhinged the brakes of the wheels to the bed. Vivienne stood up and held Marion's hand. She walked with them down the hall as they rolled the stretcher through the various wards.

Marion glanced up at Vivienne. 'If I don't make it today, you have to let me go.' The silence was finally broken; Marion had snapped back into a lucid state. There had been plenty of time to speak on the way to the hospital. Or before the anaesthetist's speech that almost put them to sleep. Why now, when they were seconds away from entering the operating room?

'Please. Stop,' Vivienne whispered and turned away from her mother, knowing that if she entertained the thought, tears would start flooding her eyes.

Marion tugged on her fingers. 'Don't look away from me, Vivienne, please.' The stretcher slowed down, suddenly coming to a halt, stopped by two large white doors with silver handles.

'You had all this time, Mama. All this time to say something.'

'Sorry, but this as far as you can go,' one of the staff said, seemingly eager.

'Just know that I will always watch over you.' Before she could respond, the stretcher had been pushed past the threshold, away into the operating room. Vivienne wasn't religious in the slightest, yet at that moment, she prayed. Prayed that she would see her mother again. Prayed that those weren't the last moments spent with her. That was the thing about *last times*—they usually sped by, unnoticed. If people knew when they were experiencing *the last time,* would they have savoured it more? Cherished the moment and sunk their teeth in, enjoying every last bite? But people were too busy chasing illusions to stop and think about what was right in front of them. Forgetting the past was too easy. Vivienne dwelled on these uncomfortable thoughts, and she couldn't decide whether it was healthy. When was the last time she tasted her grandmother's cooking? When was the last time she rode her bicycle with Thomas? The answers were somewhere locked deep within her mind.

The wait had exceeded three hours. A nurse regularly came in and notified them about Marion's state—which, for the most part was good, as far as they knew. Adrion rested on Vivienne's shoulder while she wrote in her notebook. She needed to distract herself. Her writing allowed her to escape into another world. It was between that or pacing the hospital hallways for hours on end. However, her writing entailed death and tragedy, trapping her. Since her surroundings were filled with misery, it manifested itself into the chapters of her novel.

'We should go for a walk. Take your mind off things,' Adrion said spontaneously, lifting his head from her shoulder.

'I can't leave her.'

'How about we go out and get her something nice to wake up to?' Adrion suggested, assuredly. Vivienne closed the notebook and slid it into her satchel. She knew Marion would appreciate waking up to a gift, something that would lift her morale.

'I suppose we could pick up some flowers for her. There's a florist down the road.' As a child, her mother was obsessed with flowers. Each table in the house had a vase with some form of flora sticking out of it. Leaves, twigs, vines—and everything else imaginable—included. The place was never monotonous, that was certain. The florist was only a few blocks down from the hospital, an undeniably tremendous location. Most florists only made significant sales during specific times of the year, for instance, Valentine's Day and other trivial events. But when positioned only doors away from a hospital, the opportunities were endless. There was never a shortage of sick and dying people who needed cheering up.

When Vivienne stepped into the shop, the aromas impaled her nostrils. She had forgotten how overwhelming the scent was.

'Do you know what type of flowers Marion likes?'

'The more appropriate question is which flowers *doesn't* she like.' Vivienne stood still and looked around. 'I think I'll know when I see them.' She spun her head, checking to see if anything caught her eye. With some careful consideration, she approached a set of flowers and picked them up. She looked at them intensely. They were predominately black with rich violet edges.

'What do you think about these ones?' She pulled the flowers out of the water and revealed them to Adrion.

'Not sure that they're suitable in this instance.'

'And how would you know what's *suitable*?' she said, quickly realising that Adrion would, in fact, know. His mum, Sofia, was a florist.

'Viv, my mum's a florist. I think I would know a thing or two about flowers.' Adrion smirked. He had worked countless summers helping his mother at the shop. The topic had been brought up in conversation several times before.

'Yes, I know that.' She teased, in an attempt to play off her forgetfulness.

'All I'm saying is that I'm *almost* certain the flowers you're holding are black dahlias. And if I'm not mistaken, they symbolise death and betrayal. Probably not something you want to bring into a hospital.' What were the chances she was attracted to the flowers that conveyed death? She didn't exactly believe in bad omens, but it would've been arrogant to go against Adrion's judgement, and tonight was not the time to jinx anything.

'Oh,' she uttered, as she placed the flowers down. She scanned the room a second time, hoping to find something that was equally as appealing. She had never appreciated the colour pink; it was too potent. And, as she had described it, 'too in your face'. But the pastel pink flowers before her were magnificent.

'What about these?' Vivienne called out to Adrion, who was in a different section of the room now.

He wandered over to where she was pointing. 'My knowledge is a bit rusty, but I believe those are carnations. They symbolise love, and pride, and all that type of stuff . . . And I'm pretty sure the pink ones correlate to the love of a mother. Or at least people always bought them on Mother's Day.' Adrion's familiarity with the flowers was impressive, and his subtle passion for something so delicate was attractive. That, or he was making everything up. Either way she was sold.

'Well, I guess we're getting these.' Vivienne walked to the front counter and placed the bouquet down. The lady took the flowers and wrapped them in a thin white piece of paper, then a large sheet of cellophane. For the finishing touch, she added a bow. It was perfect. Vivienne was glad Adrion had coaxed her out of the hospital; the fumes of death were insufferable. He always succeeded in making a terrible situation manageable.

They entered the front doors of the hospital, took the elevator to the second level, and returned to the waiting room. As Vivienne settled into her chair and reached for her notebook, a nurse headed their direction. It was the same one that had been updating them on Marion's surgery throughout the evening. Except this time, she was approaching with purpose. Vivienne's mind instantly assumed the worst possible scenario. Her mother was dead.

'We tried to find you sooner.' The words flooded the room. Vivienne braced herself. 'There were some complications during the surgery . . . They're stabilising your mother now, but they were unable to complete it.' Saliva ran down Vivienne's throat, choking her. She didn't feel relieved, she felt sick.

'Thank you,' Adrion stepped in and said.

'The doctor will be here shortly to discuss your mother's condition further.'

'Do you think she'll be alright?' Vivienne said, finally locating her voice.

The nurse sighed. Her face was filled with pity. She must have had to deal with countless people in the same position as herself, frantic family members, hoping their loved ones would survive.

'It's not my place to say, but as far as I know, they managed to remove a large part of the cancer.'

'That's good, right?' A glimpse of hope hurtled out.

'Yes, it's good. But the fact that they had to close up early is not ideal.' Suddenly, the pager tied to the nurse's waist started to buzz. 'I have to go, sorry.' Before Vivienne had the chance to ask another question, she was gone.

Eventually, the doctor emerged. He walked over to the reception area, where a lady pointed him towards Vivienne and Adrion. He rotated his head and gave them a small wave. It wasn't much of a wave, but more an acknowledgment of their existence. The doctor marched over to where they were seated and gave an unsympathetic attempt at a smile.

'Hi. I'm one of the doctors that performed the surgery on your mother this evening,' he clarified. 'As I'm sure you've been made aware, we ran into some complications. There was some internal bleeding that caused her to become unstable and we couldn't allow her to go into cardiac arrest. We managed to remove a large portion of the cancerous area, but not all of it. I have never seen such an aggressive tumour. It was quite something . . . After she recovers, we can look at possible options for treatment.' The doctor was so blunt. He didn't show a scrap of compassion, acting like Marion was just a hunk of meat. There was no doubt, he was more interested in the intricacy of the cancer than her survival. Vivienne wanted to express her dissatisfaction but decided to bite her tongue.

'When can we see her?' she asked.

'You can see her in a moment. I'll have someone take you to her,' the doctor said and quickly left. A hospital attendant came over to where they were seated and told them to follow him. While they walked, Vivienne heard violent coughing from one of the rooms, and further down, someone was vomiting. They entered the recovery ward where Marion was. It was peaceful. A single pin could've dropped, and the sound would have resonated without disruption. Every patient was either waiting for the anaesthetic to wear off or too drained to make a sound.

'You and your sister can wait here,' the attendant whispered to Adrion. Vivienne could tell that he was trying to hide his grin.

'Thank you,' he replied. She never thought that she and Adrion could pass for siblings, but when she really considered the idea, she could see some similarities. They both had a similar intensity in their eyes. Adrion, however, had fuller lips whereas Vivienne's were thinner and cupid bowed. She was nit-picking their similarities, attempting to justify the man's comment. Maybe they didn't look alike after all.

Vivienne looked over her mother, somewhat expecting her to wake up. After glancing at her stiff body, she kissed her forehead and sat in the seat next to her, patiently waiting.

Adrion had fallen asleep. Vivienne was exhausted but fought the urge to close her eyes. After a while, Marion's eyes began to flicker. 'Vivienne?' A muffled moan fought its way out. Vivienne stood up and crouched next to her mother as she regained consciousness.

'I'm right here.'

'Did they get it all out?' she murmured, still in a haze. Vivienne didn't want to tell her mother about the complications, but she knew it would be better coming from her mouth rather than the cold doctor's.

'There were some complications. Apparently, you had some internal bleeding. They had to close up early.' A disapproving, elongated sigh lingered from Marion's lips. She was too weak to say anything. 'The good news is they managed to get a fair bit of it out,' Vivienne said, giving her mother at least something to cling onto.

'That's good, I guess.'

'You're weak at the moment, though, so get some rest. Adrion and I are going to stay the night, keep you company.'

Marion tilted her head to the side and looked at the small desk in the corner of the room. 'Pink carnations.' Her dry, cracked lips began to bleed from the smile that ran across her face. 'Those are my favourite.'

'Adrion helped me pick them, I just kind of watched.' Vivienne took the flowers and placed them in Marion's lap.

'You caught a good one. Gentle, that's rare.' Nestling her nose into the bouquet, she sniffed the flowers. Vivienne couldn't tell whether her mother was referring to Adrion or the bouquet.

Adrion, she presumed. 'Now all we need is a nice vase to accompany them.'

'Don't worry, Mama, I'll go out tomorrow and find any vase you desire . . . Just rest now.' Vivienne stroked her mother's head and went back to her seat. She kissed Adrion gently on the lips, just with enough pressure to leave his sleep uninterrupted. Her mother was right, she had caught a good one.

CHAPTER SIXTEEN

The varnished wooden desk, her safe haven. Vivienne had put a sizeable dent into the progress of her novel. Every corner of her life demanded time, time she thought she didn't have, but when she reduced the hours spent procrastinating and carrying out pointless chores, it seemed the days were almost endless. She needed someone to read her writing with fresh eyes, someone who could validate her progress. But who? The first two candidates that came to mind were Hugo and Professor Clarke. She contemplated showing Hugo, but he was too nice and had the tendency to sugar-coat things. Which would've been fine if she were looking to make her secretly big ego bigger. What Vivienne needed was someone objective, and Professor Clarke was perfect. She knew what she had written was good. More than good, it was brilliant, the concept down to the minute details. However, to truly give her writing purpose, she needed someone to read it, otherwise her motivation, and ideas, would likely wither away.

Marion had recovered well from the surgery, very well. The type of well Vivienne hadn't expected. There had been talk of another round of chemotherapy. Vivienne wasn't opposed, but apprehensive. She had seen what the chemo did to her mother—made her so terribly sick. But if the medical 'professionals' advised more chemo, there was little she could do about it. They were at their whims.

Vivienne laid on the couch, in her hand a book. *A Maid's Tale* was the title. It was an autobiography about a woman that was part of a long, generational line of maids—'maids' because the word 'slaves' was too daunting—who took care of an affluent family. Far more affluent than Amelie's family. The premise of Vivienne's novel involved a maid who finds herself entangled in forbidden love. The novel toggled between the maid's point of view and the perspective of her lover, sometimes in the form of letters. As Vivienne read the novel, the lines started to fuse together. Her eyesight had progressively gotten worse, and she had prompted herself to see a specialist, but she never managed to get around to it. There was a creaking sound coming from what she believed were the floorboards. Although when she tuned in closer, she could tell she was mistaken. A light flickered in her mind and a case of déjà vu coursed through her. She ran to the balcony doors and stared down. There he was, Adrion, throwing tiny stones at her window.

'I'll be down in a second.' Vivienne smiled at him. She folded the corner of the book, closed it, and proceeded to rummage through her closet. She tugged the clothes off their hangers, paving a way to it—Marion's white dress. Vivienne pulled the clothes to one side, revealing the garment in full. It hadn't been touched since her first night with Adrion.

'So where are we going tonight?'

Adrion examined her, the single dimple appearing faintly on his cheek. 'The infamous white dress. Hope you don't mind getting it scuffed.' He grabbed her waist and kissed her. Vivienne knew exactly where they were heading, and she didn't mind if she scuffed the dress, as long as she was with him. The thought of their first kiss often entered her mind. The feeling of being touched—actually touched—was so euphoric that she thought she might melt. When they arrived, they circled the perimeter of the gardens, rolled the log that somehow hadn't moved, and vaulted over the brick wall. The grounds of the garden had an otherworldly brilliance during the night. The trees felt like an entity hovering over her, whispering sweet nothings. She closed her eyes and allowed herself to be taken.

'You can open your eyes now.' Adrion slowly stopped and let go of Vivienne's hand. Vivienne's eyelids rose vigilantly, as if somebody were hiding, prepared to scare her.

'Oh my . . . You've outdone yourself,' she said in awe. Spread along the grass was a chequered picnic blanket, a silver lantern, and a long, wooden board with an assortment of fruits, cheeses, and cured meats. Knowing Adrion, she knew there would've also been a bottle of wine in close proximity.

'Glad you're impressed. The guy at the deli almost did his back getting this ready by tonight. The things I do for you, Vivienne.' Adrion directed her to sit down. 'I know that your life has been complicated lately. You've been through a lot these past couple of months, and every time you're knocked down, you come back fighting. It's admirable, honestly. I wanted to do something special tonight, and here I hold some of my fondest memories with you.'

'Adrion, this is perfect.' Vivienne stood and tossed her arms over his shoulders and squeezed.

'Enough of my ranting—let's sit down. Enjoy some cheese and I'll get the wine.' He stood up and retrieved the bottle. He could be so predictable.

It didn't take them long to finish the spread, or the wine. The night became crisp as the cover of clouds vanished. Vivienne hadn't thought far enough ahead to bring a jacket. In the spirit of resourcefulness, Adrion cleared the picnic blanket and folded half over them, like a cocoon. Vivienne looked over at him and took his arm, angling it upwards.

'That's Aries,' she said, guiding his hand in a curved motion.

A small laugh shot from Adrion's mouth. 'Hey, don't go stealing my moves.'

'Our moves, you mean.' Adrion's face soothed as the words warmed the sky.

It was the day of Marion's review. The doctor assigned to her case was no longer Doctor Dupont; it was someone else more suited to her unique circumstances.

'Hi, Mama.' Vivienne walked into the hospital room. Marion was sitting up, reading the newspaper. There wasn't much to do other than read and complain about the food. Her mother had become overly worried about the management of the bookstore. She trusted the four people she had hired, but no one could tend to the needs of the store like she could. Marion insisted that Vivienne go to the store at least every second day. Her mother had told her to be a 'little spy' and report back to her with any news. It was a bookshop, though, not a circus, so naturally, there was little to report. The only truly interesting things in the shop were within the pages of the books, but nevertheless, she carried out her mother's request. Because if Marion lost her sanity, Vivienne knew she would have been irrefutably close behind.

'Hey, Viv. I think Doctor Deger will be here in a moment.' Before Marion could add anything, the doctor waltzed into the room with a nurse trailing behind. Vivienne had had an interaction with Doctor Deger once before. He walked a fine line between confident and completely up himself. He was attractive, though, it had to be handed to him. The people who made him must have been blessed with the genes of Aphrodite. She could tell her mother had a little crush by the way she tilted her head and nodded to what he was saying. Doctor Deger had the eye candy effect, which masked practically all of an individual's flaws, from their intellectual capabilities to their social abilities. Vivienne had learnt quite early on that life was remarkably easier for attractive people. Marion was a prime example and victim of the 'eye candy' effect. All that Vivienne wanted was less suave and more medicating.

'So, the good news is that you have recovered amazingly, Marion. The swelling around your abdomen has gone down significantly and your white blood cell count is back to normal,' Doctor Deger explained, his medical talk sounding as seductive as ever. 'Now, we need to talk about the next steps. With your consent, we believe that we should proceed with another round of chemo. We may not get another chance if we don't act soon. The window of opportunity is closing.' Vivienne may not have had a doctorate in medicine, but it didn't take a genius to realise Marion was still fragile. The doctor had a point, however. Time was of the essence.

'I hate to interrupt. I know it's not my place to say, but don't you think another round of chemo is incredibly risky?' the nurse interjected. Vivienne appreciated that she was advocating for her mother.

'Yes, you are right—it's not your place. The 'Dr' in my name stands for 'I know what I'm doing'. The fact of the matter is that if we don't try to eradicate the cancer now, the chances of going into remission will plummet,' the doctor said, with slight agitation in his voice.

'I have been looking after this patient for ten days and I believe that—'

'You are out of line. Nurse.' It was unsettling watching them argue. Vivienne utterly hated that Doctor Deger undermined the nurse in such a manner, but she had to agree with him. Marion would have rather died than not go into full remission.

'Mama, what do you want to do?' Vivienne faced her mother and questioned.

Marion turned to the doctor and nodded. 'If this will give me the best chance, I'm willing to go ahead.'

'I've seen you, Marion; you're a fighter. You've got this,' the nurse said, reassuringly. Vivienne was impressed with her maturity. If she were the nurse, she would have stuck it to Doctor Deger and maybe even given him a fist to the face.

'This does mean you'll be in the hospital for a bit longer. So, if you'd like to bring in a few more things from home to make this place more pleasant, by all means, do so,' the doctor said, then left with the nurse.

'What would you like me to get from the house?' Vivienne asked.

'I don't know. You know, just the usual.' There was not a clue in her mind to what that meant. They hadn't done this before. This wasn't a café—what was the usual?

'More specific?'

'There is one thing. Can you bring my soft bathrobe?'

'Okay. Anything else?'

'If you see something you think I might need, bring it.' Vivienne thought she might have needed to create a list of her mother's demands, but one bathrobe was manageable.

'Will do. Be back soon.' She took her coat and made her way to the black Volkswagen. Vivienne yearned for the day she never had to hear the words Marion, cancer, and chemo in the same sentence.

She parked and approached the house. Her feet slowed as if she were trudging through wet cement. A man with buzzed hair posed at her front door, arms crossed with one leg against the wall. There was no one at home. Louis was working, and Marion was bedridden in hospital. Who was this stranger?

Standing there, just out of sight behind the fence, she stared at him. He was yet to notice her. She stared intensely, trying to confirm whether she was hallucinating, but she wasn't. The birthmark behind his left ear was too recognisable. She wondered how it was possible.

'Thomas?' she called out. The man slowly turned around.

'Vivienne?' It was him. His voice was the same, but deeper. His head was shaven, his shoulders were broader, and he had finally grown into himself. Under his changes, she could still see her beloved Thomas, home, like a soldier returning from war. She never thought she would lay eyes on him again. It took her years to accept it, but now he had returned. As she ran towards him, time began to warp. She felt like a child again, running into the safety of his arms. With one giant leap, she latched onto him. The ecstasy that coursed through her was inconceivable.

'How the fuck are you here right now?' She pinched him.

'Ouch!' Thomas laughed. 'Where do I even begin? Well, I needed to come to Paris for some things and the minute I landed, I rushed over here. I was scared you'd changed your address, but I had a look through the window and saw your baby picture on the mantel piece.' Vivienne still had difficulty comprehending the situation.

'Marion is going to go wild when she sees you. I still can't believe it—how is this possible? Also, I can't emphasise this enough, you're an arsehole for leaving me.' The sentences spilled out from her mouth. Her brain was still in sensory overload, and she was struggling to maintain basic functioning.

'I was stupid, Viv. I should have explained everything before I left, but at the time, I thought it would've been easier if I didn't. Mum took us with barely any notice. I wanted to contact you, I really did, but I didn't know how. Mum had already severed all connections to France by then . . . Too many bad memories, she said.' Under his slightly serious tone, she could tell that he was just as elated to see her, if not more.

'And how are Maxim and Camille?' Those were Thomas's siblings. Camille was the oldest and Maxim the youngest, leaving Thomas caught in the middle.

'They're good, good. Maxim has almost finished school and Camille moved to England, so we don't see much of her.'

'England. Nice.'

'Mum didn't want her to go, but she was adamant. Anyways, where's Marion?' Vivienne didn't know how to break the news to him without destroying the triumphant feeling of their reunion.

'She's in the hospital.'

'Oh, why?'

'Cancer.' Thomas gave a heavy sigh. He had been through the heartache before of losing someone to cancer. 'But she would love to see you. What's your schedule like?'

'Honestly, I have a heap of time on my hands.'

'Well, she has to stay in the hospital for a few more weeks. Drop by anytime that suits, really.'

'Definitely. And how about we get dinner later?'

'I would love that.'

Vivienne and Thomas had known one another ever since they were children. But before they were friends, they were merely acquaintances. She lived exactly twelve doors down from him. He rode his bicycle to school every day. Vivienne, on the other hand, walked. One afternoon, after school had ended, she asked—practically begged—her mother for a bicycle. Seeing Thomas rocketing past her had trigged something hidden within her. Maybe it was her competitive nature, or maybe Thomas just intrigued her. It was fascinating to Vivienne that he was one of the most consistent things within her life, a variable that never changed, yet she knew so little about him. Who was this boy?

Soon enough, she began riding. He noticed, of course. Gradually, she rode closer to him, until one day, she decided to ride next to him. Two weeks passed and neither of them spoke. Nothing had changed; it was as if she were still walking. But then he acknowledged her.

'I'm Thomas,' he said.

'I know,' she replied.

When Vivienne first properly met Thomas, he was shy and timid, but as their friendship blossomed over the years, he changed. Maybe Vivienne brought him out of his shell. But how? She, at the time, was just as shy as he was. Possibly the realisation that he had someone by his side was enough for him to evolve into the person he became. Vivienne loved every stage of him. Sometimes, people changed for the worse, but Thomas's change was neither bad nor good. It was just change.

Vivienne walked over to a table wedged in the corner of the restaurant, where Thomas was seated. 'Wow. You look gorgeous tonight,' he said, analysing her.

When they were younger, they had an ongoing joke. Whenever they went out to a café or restaurant together, they would sit at the table closest to the rear of the room. While eating their food, they would watch the other customers and try to unpack their lives—like a private investigator. They would examine their clothing, accents, accessories, and other peculiar features. After, they would determine who they were, allowing their imaginations to run rampant. The theories progressively became wilder, and Vivienne always found herself in stitches from laughing. She couldn't gather whether he had picked the table at the restaurant as part of their ongoing jest, or if it was just a sweet coincidence.

'You're also looking rather fine. Some might call you a stud.'

Vivienne chuckled.

'Stop, you're making me blush,' he replied, matching her energy.

She took her seat and filled their glasses with water. 'So much to unpack . . . Give me a brief, but not too brief, summary of everything that has happened from the day you left until now,' Vivienne said, staring at him eagerly. She had an insatiable desire to know about his life. Deprived of his company for so long, there was a need to quench her thirst. She needed to know—what could four years do to a person?

'As you know, we left and moved to Canada. My English was terrible at first, but I picked it up fairly quickly. I hated the place, but you get used to it. I took an interest in medicine after my father died, and in my final year, I decided that's what I wanted to study. And that's what I did . . . well, am doing.' It was great information, but awfully vanilla. She wanted the gruesome details.

'Any love interests?' she enquired.

'There was one girl I met at university. Her name's Amanda. But things didn't end well. She was part of the reason I came here.' Vivienne felt odd. But why? Was it jealousy? But why would she be jealous? She knew exactly why. However, the truth was too much to bear. She tried to suppress the emotions, which she successfully did for many years. But the past found a way to reinstate those dormant feelings. A few months before Thomas and his family left for Canada, there was a moment. A kiss. Vivienne always loved Thomas, but as she matured, she realised the love she felt wasn't platonic. She thought it was an unrequited type of love, a one-sided love. But everything changed when his lips warmed hers. When he left, not only did she lose her closest friend, but she also lost something that never had the chance to begin. Their connection, a foetus that never made it to term.

As the dinner continued, Vivienne told Thomas about Amelie and their complex relationship. She also talked about her time at the university, briefly mentioning Adrion, however somehow failing to declare their relationship status. The conversation between them ceased temporarily as Vivienne took a sip of her wine.

'What do you think about that guy?' Vivienne glanced over her shoulder and followed Thomas's eyes. He was very cunning; where they were seated wasn't a coincidence.

'I knew you didn't choose this table by chance.' Vivienne smirked and brought her attention back to the man. 'He is "unhappily" married with a pain-in-the-arse wife and three kids. And the girl across from him is either his eldest daughter or his assistant that he's sleeping with,' Vivienne said.

Thomas mirrored her smirk. 'You read my mind.'

Vivienne pulled a loose watch from her pocket. 'I should get going.'

'Let me drive you.'

'Are you sure?'

'Yes, I'm sure,' he replied. They both left the restaurant and walked to Thomas's rental car. 'When are you free next, Viv?' he asked as they turned into her street.

'Whenever. Surprise me.' As they approached, Adrion was waiting at the front. He looked up and squinted his eyes with suspicion. Thomas parked the car, walked around, and opened Vivienne's door. Locking eyes with Adrion, she could feel an awkward energy burst through the air like shrapnel, flooding the atmosphere, leaving nothing but an uncomfortable silence.

'Thomas, this is Adrion. Adrion, Thomas.' Vivienne acquainted them. 'Thomas is the old friend I mentioned. The one that lives in Canada.' Adrion's face slightly soothed, his guard still up. Vivienne knew how it must've seemed, coming home with a man he had never met. Thomas also seemed confused. She told him about Adrion, but never explicitly stated their relationship. Vivienne turned and faced Thomas. 'And this is my boyfriend.'

'Oh, yes. You talked about him at the restaurant,' he replied. 'Nice to meet you, Adrion.'

'You too.' The tension had settled. The area reeked of testosterone; behind their eyes, they were territorial.

'I'll see you later, Thomas,' she said, as they exchanged a wave.

'He seems . . . nice,' Adrion said, as if he were held at gun point. Vivienne could sense some unrest. Thomas was the past. It was nice to reminisce, yet she loved Adrion. He was the present, the future, right?

CHAPTER SEVENTEEN

'Professor Clarke,' Vivienne called out as the lecture room emptied.

'Vivienne, glad to see you back in class,' she replied and wandered over to Vivienne, who was seated in the second row from the front. 'How's your mother?'

'She's . . .' Silence fell, as she searched for an appropriate word. 'Coping.' Marion's condition was consistent, which was good in the sense that she wasn't getting worse. 'The doctors are proceeding with another round of chemotherapy. They told us it's her best chance.'

'I'm pleased to see you holding up.'

A shy, dismissive smile crept onto Vivienne's face. 'Anyways, I wanted to talk to you about something.' She unbuckled her bag and pulled out a stack of paper, bound by a paper clip positioned on the top left corner. 'I've been working on a project.'

'What kind of project?' The professor unfolded the glasses in her hand and placed them over her eyes. With one swift movement, she swiped the manuscript off the desk and flicked through the pages. 'What is this?'

'It's the first few chapters of the novel I'm writing.'

'A novel, how exiting. Took my advice, I see.' Professor Clarke had told Vivienne 'pen to paper', so that was precisely what she had done. 'You would like me to read it, I presume?'

'If it's not too much trouble.' Professor Clarke closed the manuscript and tucked it into her bag. She had unusually callused hands for someone who wrote for a living. Must have been a hefty grip she had on that pen. A weight had been lifted off Vivienne's shoulders. Although she secretly coveted the professor's approval, the courage she had built to hand in her work was enough to satisfy her.

'I'll read it over the next few days and give you my feedback. Very proud of you.'

'Thank you,' Vivienne said, then sped out the classroom, barely able to contain her excitement. She didn't want to live in a state of inertia, constantly fulfilling the same monotonous tasks. And for what? Life only gave her a finite amount of time, and she wanted every moment of it to be filled with passion. That's what she loved about writing. It was a way of moving forwards, a way to break that mundane cycle that she was secretly terrified of, and ultimately, a path to escape. Vivienne could feel her writing improving every day. Her studies at the university were undoubtably a contributing factor. She also attributed this improvement to how nomadic she had felt. She was feeling things so rich and raw that she had never experienced before. She longed for love and suddenly, it was all around her, and all she had to understand it were words. Words that now had weight and meaning and could be tied to a specific smell or sound or taste. The turmoil of her life was beautifully destructive. This destruction may not have been as beautiful if she didn't write, but writing allowed her to see the beauty in everything. The beauty of the cells multiplying in her mother's body. It was wicked and disturbing, but so poetic. Writing was like taking drugs, only better. She allowed herself to shun the world and lose herself in the pages that swayed side to side on her typewriter, like a psychedelic experience. She sometimes thought she could stay in this limbo forever, but she always came back, because no matter how much power they yielded, they were simply just words on a page.

'Vivienne!' A voice shouted from outside the university gates. She turned her head and looked down the street, trying to locate the source. Then she spotted Thomas waving his hands manically. He was wearing a bulky black helmet, and next to him was a red Vespa. It was almost impossible to recognise him, but his intoxicating spontaneity—and smile—made him hard to miss.

'What are you doing here?' she ran up to him and whispered loudly.

He took his helmet off and brushed over his non-existent hair. 'I'm taking you out.' Without another word or explanation, Thomas pulled a helmet from behind his back and placed it on Vivienne's head.

'I can't just leave, I've got stuff to do. Where are you taking me?'

'Full of questions, aren't you?' he said, as he revved the engine. 'If you must know, I'm taking you hostage and hauling you back to Canada.'

'You're so funny. Ever thought about pursuing a career in stand-up comedy? Forget medicine.'

'Fine. Such a buzzkill. I'm taking you to the Louvre, happy?'

Vivienne absolutely loved museums, but especially the Louvre. It had such a rich and profound history. It was originally built as a fortress, then served as a royal palace. In the late 18th century, it was transformed into a museum, where everyone could enjoy its beauty. She knew its entire history like the back of her hand. Vivienne first visited the Louvre when she was fourteen, as part of a school excursion. When she stepped foot into the building, she was instantly mesmerised. The corridors were filled with paintings that reached the ceilings, even paintings that spanned entire walls. She only spent a few hours at the museum, her time cut short. She expressed her disappointment to her parents that night, and a day later, there she was, back at the Louvre. Vivienne had certainly conjured up some luck in the parent department. They were always present, but it was instances like these that reminded her the never-ending extent of their generosity. Most parents would have given their child some false promise or a simple no, but not Marion and Louis.

Vivienne hadn't been on a motorcycle before, not because it frightened her, but simply because the opportunity had never arisen. It was exiting, though, having the raw wind pass through her hair, her arms tight around Thomas's waist. She wanted him to go faster so she could pretend she was scared and tighten her grip on him. Once they arrived at the museum, Thomas parked the Vespa and wrapped the two helmets around the silver handlebars.

'Even after all this time, it still takes my breath away.' He sighed and glanced at the building reflectively. 'You know, I heard that they're planning to build a pyramid, right in the centre of the courtyard.'

Vivienne turned to him, confused. 'What do you mean a pyramid?'

'I'm not sure. Just a pyramid, I guess. I think it's to attract more tourists.'

'People always want to fix what's not broken. And we already have enough tourists.' Vivienne shook her head. She couldn't understand why someone would want to interfere with hundreds of years of history.

'Well, we should enjoy it while it lasts. First it will be pyramids, next a desert.' Vivienne turned to Thomas and grinned. As they entered the museum, they were greeted by a smell she had long forgotten. A nice, sterile smell with undertones of chestnuts. They began their descent down the hallways.

Many of the paintings that they walked past depicted half-naked men and women, on the verge of death, experiencing unimaginable pain. Vivienne appreciated those paintings the most. The past was filled with vile things, which wasn't necessarily good but enabled the elements necessary to create an instinctual, life-threatening fear. Sure, people could still experience fear in the modern world, however, certainly not to the extent that the people in those paintings did. She appreciated the way museums acknowledged the past and how far humans had collectively come. Here, she was safe while finding joy in paintings of others suffering. It also seemed perverted.

'What do you think that guy is thinking?' Thomas whispered and pointed to a man in a painting, who was being bludgeoned to death. Vivienne didn't know what he would have been thinking. What did people back then think about in the moments before death? Seeing their family one last time? Living?

'I'm not sure. Steak, possibly?' Thomas let out a short laugh that echoed through the empty corridors.

'You really haven't changed.'

'Okay, my turn. What do you suppose she's thinking?' Vivienne pointed to a woman in the same painting.

'She's thinking that men are idiots.'

'And why do you think that?' she asked.

'Look how she's glaring at them. That face says, "Yes, we get it, you all have big—"' Before Thomas could finish the sentence, Vivienne raised the pamphlet in her hand and hit him. She found the comment rather amusing, but unfortunately couldn't say the same for the elderly couple that was next to them, trying to enjoy their afternoon.

Closing hour at the museum approached quickly. Time had a habit of escaping them when they were together. Vivienne's arms swayed as they walked back to the motorcycle, her fingers pulsating every time they accidently brushed against Thomas's hand. Feeling his warm skin made her weak at the knees. This greyed-out image she once had of him now had blood and flesh and witty comebacks. It was dangerous having him around. He was like the apple in the Garden of Eden. Forbidden, yet so tempting.

'Hey, call me, okay?' Thomas said as Vivienne hopped off the motorcycle.

She smiled. 'I will, but try to refrain from stalking me at the university.'

'What can I say? You're irresistible.' She could tell the difference between friendly banter and flirting, and this felt like the latter. It felt dirty, like tar, but the most awful part was that it didn't feel wrong. That's what frightened her the most.

Vivienne reached into her bag for the keys to her apartment and unlocked the door. As she walked in, she was greeted by the sound of the telephone ringing. She quickly dropped her bag and scurried to the kitchen, unaware of how long it had been drumming.

'Hello?' Vivienne said, pushing the phone against her ear.

'Hello, this is Zoe. I'm calling about your mother, Marion. I'm one of the nurses looking after her.'

'Yes, what about her? Is she alright?' She tuned in closer.

'Your mother was feeling unwell and asked that we contact you.' Vivienne wondered what 'unwell' meant. It was a vague term. Was her mother suffering from a head cold or was this serious?

'Thanks for calling. I'll be there soon.' She hung up and slipped into her shoes that she had just relieved herself of. Until that moment, she had never received a call from the hospital regarding her mother's health. It was out of the ordinary, but she persuaded herself not to panic. However, the car speedometer on the way to the hospital would have argued otherwise.

'Mama?' Vivienne said, out of breath.

'Hey, Vivi.' To her surprise, Marion was sitting up in bed, enjoying an early supper. Her mother seemed completely fine. She even had a rosy glow to her cheeks that had returned after being vacant for months.

'I got a call from one of the nurses saying you were sick,' Vivienne said, with almost a sense of disappointment. The lengthy drive was one that she had to endure plenty of times throughout the week. Unnecessary trips to the hospital were far from exhilarating.

'I was feeling unwell a couple of hours ago and lost consciousness for a bit. I asked for one of the nurses to call you, but only minutes later, I was feeling fine. They said my body was just struggling with the chemo, that's all,' Marion explained. She was calm and composed for someone who had allegedly been fighting to stay conscious.

'You gave me a heart attack.'

'I didn't mean to disturb you. I was just scared.' Vivienne couldn't argue with her mother's logic. It must have been distressing, not having herself and Louis close. Marion missed the paintings from home, the music, the books. This hospital room was killing her soul. If the shoe were on the other foot, Vivienne would have already pulled the intravenous from her arm and left guns blazing. She suddenly felt so incredibly guilty, guilty for simply living.

'I'm here now. How about I stay the night? I can read you those gossip magazines you're obsessed with. And I'll even dramatise them too,' she suggested with a grin.

'I've been getting the nurses to read them out loud, but it's just not the same.' Marion shuffled to the left side of the single foam mattress and placed her hand next to Vivienne's. 'Come sit,' she said, with a tilted head and a tiny smile.

'Just . . . don't scare me like that again.'

'Don't worry. I won't, my love.'

'I can't believe Monsieur Belan didn't think my essay was "up to standard",' Vivienne whined, as she and Adrion walked down the hallway. 'Look what he wrote,' she said, shoving the paper in front of him. 'Vivienne structured her essay correctly, however, approached her writing as an opinion piece. When making bold claims, evidence must back them up,' the small, written comment at the bottom of the page read. There was plenty of evidence, he had just decided that being an unwavering prick was his calling. She was more upset because she knew he had a personal issue with her rather than the criticism itself.

'What did he write for yours?' She peeked over at his paper.

He lifted it up and began to read aloud. 'Adrion demonstrated an excellent and nuanced understanding in his essay. He is encouraged to continue this great work.'

Vivienne lifted her eyebrows and smirked. 'Wow, look at my little shining star,' she teased. It was blatantly obvious that Monsieur Belan had a biased judgement. Nevertheless, she kept her big mouth shut in fear of sounding like a parrot.

'How does it feel to not be the smartest one in the relationship?'

'Don't let that head of yours get too big.' A hand pressed on Vivienne's shoulder. At first, she thought it was Adrion's, but as she turned her head to the side, Professor Clarke stood before her, appearing from thin air.

'Glad I caught you,' she said, then directed her attention to Adrion. 'If you're busy, I can talk to you after our next class.'

'No, this is a good time.' Vivienne faced Adrion and grabbed his hand affectionately. 'I'll meet you back at mine.' He nodded and headed for the door.

'Here, come into my office.' Vivienne entered and sat comfortably in the seat that the professor's hand was gesturing to.

'Why did you want to see me?'

'I read your manuscript, and well, to put it simply, it was brilliant.' The manuscript had already been read? Vivienne was stunned by the turnaround, and even more so that Professor Clarke had found it 'brilliant'. She sat with anticipation. She didn't expect this moment to feel so surreal. 'I also handed it in to my publisher on behalf of myself. They read it and were blown away with not only the story but the intricacy of the writing. When I explained it was one of my students that wrote it . . . let's just say they weren't far from speechless.' Vivienne, in that moment, felt as if she had been reincarnated. She never knew exactly what her life had been amounting to, but this was it. Every pen stroke, every late night, every time she felt insignificant or worthless, it was all a journey to this moment. This steppingstone. To be informed that a publisher not only read her work but was left speechless meant everything to her.

'I—I can never repay you for this, this is too much.' Vivienne stammered over each word.

'Trust me, it's nothing. You have created something beautiful that deserves to be seen. The least I can do is help you get there.' It became clear that Professor Clarke had always been there, looking over her. Not just a guiding light, but a veiled guardian angel.

'You got me the job with Hugo, and now this.' Vivienne paused. An existential question suddenly exposed itself. 'I also show up late . . . a lot . . . What I'm trying to get at is, why?'

'There is a reason I took an interest in you,' she said, while crossing her legs and interlocking her fingers. 'It's because I see myself in you. And when I was your age, I wish I had someone to push me forward. Instead, the bulk of my work stayed buried away in a locked cabinet until I was in my early thirties. They say we become wiser as we age, but all I see are brains stripped of individuality. Yours is young and agile, and as a teacher, a mentor, it is my duty to seek that spark. And you, Vivienne, are not just a spark, you're a wildfire.' Speechless. There was so much passion in the professor's voice. Every past misconception of Vivienne's character, everyone who didn't see her or believe in her, didn't matter. Because now she was finally seen by the person who mattered most. 'They want to have the first ten chapters finalised and delivered to them by Friday next week. Only if you can and want to, of course.' There was still tons of editing that awaited her. It wasn't a matter of whether she could do it—she had to.

'I'll have it to you by then, no problems. Once again, thank you.' As she stood up and left the office, she felt the overwhelming urge to share the news with someone. Two names came to mind, one after the other. Adrion and Thomas. However, not in that order. Although her mind was agile, it couldn't escape everything. A brain had two hemispheres, though—surely there was room for both of them. It was her brain; she had the right to think what she liked. Thoughts couldn't be right or wrong. Right?

CHAPTER EIGHTEEN

Narrow-mindedness and tunnel vision. She had the tendency to limit herself to see only what was in front of her, what was staring her right in the eye. Her door was locked, and her blinds open only enough to allow some sun to crawl through. The den was closed, nothing coming in or out. Well, almost nothing. Friday was approaching and Vivienne's long, ghostly fingers could only type so fast. Rewriting the first ten chapters to perfection was presenting itself as challenging. She had loved what she had written, but for some reason unbeknown to her, she also feared it. The pressure of living up to an expectation, when previously, she just wrote for the sake of writing. Waves of nausea came unexpectedly at the thought of this pressure.

She looked up from the typewriter and absorbed the sun. She had learned how to photosynthesise after giving up on food on day two. Her fridge had emptied, and she hadn't bothered to refill it, which didn't cause any distress as writing was sustenance enough. As she closed her eyes, there was a sweet and expected knock on the door. Although nothing came in or out, Thomas was the rare exception. Vivienne told him that she'd be preoccupied with other things for a few days and couldn't have any distractions—Thomas was the biggest distraction in her life. Yet he knew she had to eat. So every day around noon, there was a knock on the door, and along with it, his precious face. It was brief, but it was enough.

'What's on the menu today?' Vivienne smiled, her sleepless eyes half shut.

Thomas lifted the items from his side. 'The chef made you a prosciutto sandwich and a jar of his "world-renowned" cherry jam,' he said, mimicking the courteous persona of a butler.

'You sure know how to please a woman.' She swooped and took the food, acting as though she were dying of famine, which she was. Although her empty stomach *was* self-inflicted.

'How's the writing coming along?'

'It'll be tight, but I reckon I can have it done by Friday.'

'They're going to love it.' Thomas looked at Vivienne with admiration. 'It's kind of incredible that you're going to be able to call yourself an author soon.'

'Let's not jump the gun.'

'No, I'm serious. I remember as kids, you wouldn't shut up about your dream of writing a novel.' He began to laugh. 'I remember reading that short story you wrote. The one about the two lovers that couldn't touch because of some supernatural force.' It left her silently dumbfounded how he still remembered that story. Little did he know, it was written about him. 'You've always loved love.' He looked at her, then down at the jar of jam. 'Well, I'll let you get back to it . . . also, open a window—it feels like death in here.'

'Alright.' Vivienne chuckled, hugging him with her free hand.

'Also, don't doubt yourself.'

'What do you mean?'

'Before you said, "don't jump the gun". You're going to be an author, Vivienne, and a bloody good one at that.'

'Yeah, I know, I was just being modest.'

Thomas gave one of his cheeky grins and shook his head. 'Tell me how the jam is; I'll report back.'

'To who?'

'The chef. Who else?' he said sarcastically, still with his stupidly irresistible grin. 'Also, I'm serious about that window.'

'You've overstayed your welcome.' Grabbing his hand, she led him to the door. 'I'll see you tomorrow.'

'Not if you keep treating me like this.'

'Bye.' She closed the door slowly while waving. After the door was shut, she raced over to the kitchen and popped the lid to the jam, retrieved a small dessert spoon, and began filling her mouth with the sweet, glossy red substance. She sat back down at her desk—jar still in hand—and glued herself to the chair.

The hours started to merge into one. Time was only differentiated by light or dark, not by the hands on the clock. However, she knew it was about six-thirty. Adrion had called and checked in on her. She was good at reading people and could tell by the infrequency in his voice that he was worried about her. Sure, it wasn't healthy to be cooped up without fresh air and human contact, but she was doing what needed to be done. Thomas understood, why couldn't Adrion? The thought of him being concerned made her profusely agitated, causing mistakes to scatter through her work. She tore the piece of paper from the typewriter, then scrunched it and pulled it apart. Her mental state was deteriorating, but the deadline would not simply cease to exist. Pain was momentary, success lasted forever, she kept repeating in her head. While she recomposed herself, the phone rang next to her.

With her head in her hand, she lifted it up. 'Hello?'

'Hi, I'm calling about your mother. I'm from the hospital.' This woman sounded significantly younger than the one that called her previously. 'I was told to call you to come in.'

'How bad is it?'

'I'm not sure, I was just told to call you,' the nurse prompted her.

'Okay, I'll come as soon as I can,' Vivienne said and laid down the phone. There were only a couple of pages left in the chapter she was typing, and the last thing she needed was to lose momentum. Plus, her mother had the propensity to overreact.

Thirty minutes struck as Vivienne placed down the final piece of paper. She straightened the pile, grabbed her keys, and made her way to the car. Her legs were numb, and each step was precarious, as if her feet were made of plasticine. The writing slump that she'd been in hadn't allowed for much more than trips to the bathroom and the pantry. On top of it all, she was incredibly sleep deprived. Making it to the car was a miracle in itself.

As she arrived at the hospital and stepped out of the car, she saw Louis, her father, standing outside the entrance smoking a cigarette. Her father rarely smoked, only when he was stressed with work. And why was he standing outside?

'Dad?' Vivienne called out, but there was no reply. At first, she thought he hadn't heard her. But how was that possible? He was standing only metres away. 'Dad?' she said again, louder.

'She is dead. Your mother is dead,' Louis said, staring at Vivienne with tearless, bloodshot eyes, his voice trembling. He covered his face with the hand holding the cigarette. Vivienne looked at her father, the realisation setting in, her lungs constricting. Her legs were no longer weak. She ran through the hospital, tears slipping off her face, everything a whitened blur. She ran as if there were something at stake, but when she reached the room, there was only the inevitable. Her mother laid there dead, barely lifeless.

'I'm so sorry.' One of the nurses appeared behind Vivienne. 'We wish there was more that we could have done, but she had a DNR in place.'

'Pardon?' In a state of shock, she walked closer to her mother's body.

'Your mother asked us not to resuscitate her in the event

that her heart failed,' the nurse explained, attempting to be considerate of Vivienne's fragile state.

She slowly brought her attention back to the nurse. 'How was I not aware of this?' Her father's same bloodshot expression now copied onto her face.

'Your father was. I'm sorry.' Vivienne picked up Marion's fingers and placed them against her cheek. They were still warm, still swimming with life. But she was gone. 'Your mother also asked us to give this to you in case she passed and you weren't here.' The nurse dug into her pocket and pulled out an unsealed envelope. The realisation had only just fully hit her. She missed her own mother's death. She was so selfish that she missed the final moments with the person she loved the most. The person who loved her the most. The person who would die for her. The person who would give the skin off their back, the ribs from their chest, and the blood from their heart. And she couldn't spare a second of her time. Only then did she realise how precious time was, and how the world had no mercy for selfish people. She didn't know what to do or what to say. And she knew she didn't deserve her mother. She didn't deserve such a beautiful soul and the universe had made that clear. Anyone who was this selfish was wretched. She wanted to kill herself. Opening the envelope took the strength of every atom in her body.

> *My dearest Vivienne,*
>
> *I am writing this letter from my room. There is a man across the road cleaning the gutters of his roof. I never realised how beautiful their home was. The surgery is tomorrow and I'm afraid something will go wrong, and I have a pit in my stomach. I don't want to worry you, so I am writing this letter instead. I remember when I first laid my eyes on you and your*

little feet. I dream about it a lot, those first few days in the hospital. I had you all to myself back then. It was as if the outside world didn't exist. I hope that's what death is like, that quiet room with you and me. Watching you grow into the strong, independent woman you are today gave purpose to a life that often felt meaningless. You were such an inquisitive kid, always wanting to know more. I know that if you could've spent all day in the bookstore, you would've. You gave me a reason to fight these past years. This world will bruise you, but to get up every day and continue is true strength. When I die, I will watch over you and keep you safe, because that's what a mother does, and one day, I hope you have the joy of experiencing it. When you try to find me when I'm gone, don't look for me in the sky—smell me in your cooking, feel me in the ocean. I love you eternally, my sweet Vivienne, forever alive.

Mama

Vivienne released the tears from her eyes, letting them stain the letter. As she slid it back into the envelope, another piece of paper poked out. It was a small card with a picture of the beach. At the top, it said 'look where I am' in Marion's distinct handwriting. A small chuckle slipped out and drifted through the dead and sterile room. She turned around and looked at her mother one last time, contemplating holding her again, but she was gone. All that remained was a soulless husk.

After passively listening to the nurse for a while, Vivienne was free to leave. Her father was still beside the entrance, smoking another cigarette.

'She was crying for you,' he said as she wandered towards him. 'I loved your mother more than anything, and she loved you more than anything.' Her eyes were puffy, and she stared soullessly at her father. 'I can't forgive you for this,' he scoffed, as he flicked the cigarette onto the floor and smothered it with the heel of his shoe.

'For what?' It was a stupid question. She already knew.

Louis draped his coat over his forearm and looked Vivienne dead in the eye, less melancholy, now with fury. 'For missing your own mother's death. For abandoning your family. I don't know you, Vivienne, and I don't want to know this person you have become. This greed inside you—it's disgusting.' His voice shuddered again. 'I don't want to see you.' Before she had the chance to defend herself, he was at the door of his car, his own getaway vehicle.

That night, when Vivienne arrived at her half home, she didn't weep or wail. Instead, she laid there, on the carpet, curled in a ball, gripping to every last fibre. Her nails dug into her hands so desperately in an attempt to ground herself. Because that night, all she wanted to do was be with her mother.

The sun rose and so did her eyes, but that was all. Her body was stiff and stuck. Her will to live was barren. Then there was a shadow, a tall figure that crept up the walls. It hovered over her for a few seconds, then collapsed and cradled her.

'I'm here.' A whisper left Adrion's mouth as he shuffled against her.

'Please don't leave me.'

'I won't.'

She didn't know how or when, but the manuscript was ready. Walking through the university, she didn't feel proud or ecstatic, because it was contaminated by the cost it came at. No amount of praise or success could mask the loss she faced.

'Professor Clarke.' Vivienne knocked on the side of the office.

'There it is' the professor said as she eyed the manuscript. 'Didn't doubt you for a second. Congratulations.' She patted

Vivienne's shoulder, then continued. 'Get prepared to have the completed manuscript ready. My instincts tell me my friends at the firm will be patiently waiting on standby.'

'I'll try my best.' An insincere smile stuck on her face.

The professor clenched her lips and placed down the script. 'Is everything alright?' she asked.

'Yes, I'm fine . . . just sleep deprived.' She laughed softly. She wasn't alright—she and 'alright' were not even on the same spectrum, but she couldn't handle the professor's pity, not then. Not ever.

'Understandable. Get some rest.' Professor Clarke moseyed back towards her desk. 'But also start preparing,' she said with keenness. 'Great things are coming.'

It certainly didn't seem that way though.

CHAPTER NINETEEN

'I've talked with my team and we're on schedule to have the flowers there by noon. We did have a slight hiccup and had to replace some of the white roses with carnations. I hope that's okay?' Sofia clarified in a soft tone. Vivienne nodded, engrossed in picking a loose seam on her dress. 'I know it's probably little consolation, but you can come to me, any time. No matter what,' she said, as she embraced Vivienne. 'Sometimes, bad things happen to good people. The world can be cruel like that.' Vivienne stood there, listening, however unable to respond. Today was the day her mother returned to the ground, and there wasn't anything to say to this. It was unfathomable to think that she could never touch her mother's face or hear her voice again. She sat there desperately trying to remember everything about her, scared the years would take these memories away from her. Time would scamper along. One day, Vivienne would be at the peak of the mountain, looking down on her life—her mother's face, then, would be a mere silhouette.

'I don't know if I'm ready,' she finally said after minutes of silence.

'I don't think this is something anyone is ever ready for.'

Sofia had been kind enough to help arrange the flowers for the funeral, free of cost. With Vivienne's father missing in action, the burden of the funeral had fallen on her shoulders. She had slipped him an envelope with the information for the service a few days prior. It was safe to assume he would attend. The chances of him speaking to her were slim, however. There had been much preparation leading to the funeral. Her aunts and uncle were both shocked and devastated by the news. It turned out that Marion had sheltered them from the extent of her condition, just as she tried to do originally to Vivienne. She couldn't decide whether this was noble or cowardly. As far as they were aware, the cancer had been eradicated 'months ago'. Maybe Marion had had false hope and was too embarrassed when her condition worsened. Earlier that week, Adrion had taken her coffin shopping, which was like grocery shopping, only more grim. Certain days were better than others. Some days, she went out, even wrote. But most days, she laid curled up in bed, like a foetus waiting to be reborn.

It had struck noon when Adrion walked down the stairs, ready in his pitch-black suit. All black suited him. He looked like a well-mannered panther. Vivienne was wearing a maroon-coloured dress. She considered wearing black but didn't want to do Marion a disservice. Marion hated black at funerals, explaining to Vivienne when she was younger that a funeral should have been a celebration of the person's life, and black didn't feel like a celebration. Maroon was the perfect balance between sweet and morbid.

'I can't believe she's gone.' A sigh left her mouth, so soft, she wondered if she had spoken at all. She stared out the window of Adrion's car and watched the droplets of rain merge into one another. It was funeral weather, she thought.

'Me neither . . .' he said, mirroring her tone. 'Did you manage to sort out the staffing issue at the store?'

'They said they're happy to stay as long as needed. I'm thinking of seeing if some can work permanently. I have to talk to Louis about it, but I can't even get a hold of him. And the place is falling apart. I don't even want to think about that right now.' Vivienne felt overwhelmed by the thought. Marion was the glue that held them together, and now, without her, every-thing was falling apart in front of her eyes.

'You should spend more time there, feel more connected to her,' Adrion suggested. Vivienne liked the idea and stored it in the back of her mind.

'Yeah, that would be nice.'

Once they arrived, it didn't take long for people to start entering through the doors. Vivienne knew most of the faces that entered, but some were unfamiliar. Marion was well trav-elled and well liked, especially in her younger years, and the numbers reflected that. People came up to Vivienne and gave their condolences. Many also felt the urge to tell her how much she had grown, and how she looked like her mother. She always thought she looked more like her father. Thomas entered. She had never seen him so sombre.

'Viv.' He stepped forward and hugged her. 'I came to bring you lunch and you weren't there, and I tried calling but you didn't answer. And when I heard the news that Marion had passed . . . I'm sorry,' Thomas said under his breath. His eyes were water coloured and beautiful under the light; he was pretty when he cried.

'I'm sorry, I was at Adrion's.'

'Don't be sorry, it's just good to see that you're alright. Well, as alright as you can be, I guess. You don't deserve this. No one does, but especially not you, especially not Marion,' Thomas said, then pulled out a neatly folded piece of paper from the front pocket of his suit. 'I also prepared something to say. If that's okay?'

'You're more than welcome.' Vivienne grabbed his hand. He nodded and took a seat close to the front of the church. As she watched Thomas take his seat, Louis snuck past. She only managed to catch a glimpse of him, but it was comforting to know he was there. The stream of people lessened, and Vivienne had a small moment to admire the church. At the back of the room was an arch-shaped, stain-glass window, and beneath it was the coffin her mother lay cold in. Individual seats were symmetrically aligned, creating fourteen rows. Flowers entertained both the entrance and the back of the church. As far as funerals went, it wasn't bad, and for a fleeting moment, she felt at peace. At peace that this funeral she had planned eased the agony of not saying goodbye, even if it only eased a fraction of this burning pain.

The room settled and there was silence. Vivienne stood from her seat and walked to the front. Initially, she thought she would be nervous, but she wasn't. She wanted everyone to know, to remember the name Marion LaRue.

'We are gathered here today to mourn as well celebrate the life of Marion,' Vivienne began to speak. 'Many of you may have only recently been made aware that she had cancer. She fought, but she lost.' Her words, although not deliberate, came out ruthless. 'Many of you know her as a friend, or sister, or lover, but she was my mother. As far as mothers went, she was perfect, perfect in every way. And I could come up here and tell you that Marion was great and perfect, but there wouldn't be much use in that. Everyone who's here knew her and knew the kind soul that was encased within. I could reminisce about the time we baked cakes. Or the time we drove five hours just to let the salt of the ocean prune our skin.' Her voice started to shake. 'But I'd rather everyone take a moment and think of your fondest memory of her. Once you have it, keep it, and every time you think of her, think of that moment. Not the cancer. Or who she left behind. Just that moment, and that moment only . . .' She could feel herself about to break down. 'I love you, Mama, and I'm sorry I wasn't a better daughter towards the end.' Her words lingered. As she went to take her seat, she could see some perplexed looks scattered throughout the church. Her speech may not have been conventional, but she had said what she had thought, and she didn't see the need to be apologetic for it. She felt a lightness when she sat back down, as though her speech wasn't a eulogy but a confession. The next eulogy read was by Marion's eldest sister. It was nice, long winded. Everything a eulogy was meant to be. There was also a childhood friend that spoke. Vivienne had never heard of her, however. A part of her expected her father to stand up, but he didn't. Finally, Thomas stood up and stepped to the front. He took the loose sheet of folded paper from his pocket, glanced at it, then placed it back.

'Growing up, I spent a copious amount of time with Vivienne. When I say copious, I mean we were practically conjoined at the hip.' The crowd let out a small collective laugh. 'By default, I also ended up spending a lot of time in the LaRue household. It was a magical place to be, always so beautifully decorated and warm. A home away from home. But Marion was what made it truly great. She was like a second mother to me. She made sure my stomach was always full; she bandaged me up when I did something stupid. She had the capacity to treat me as her own, which meant we did get in a fair few arguments. With my short temper and Vivienne's attitude, it's hard to believe she survived those years.' Thomas took a moment from his speech. His joyous tone diminished. 'Now, when I think about how safe I felt with Marion, it's hard to believe that she's gone. It has been a true honour to have her as part of my life.' He turned his head, looked at Vivienne, and smiled. A wave of memories from their childhood entered her mind, long forgotten. How had she lived without him?

Soon after Thomas's eulogy, the church service concluded. Vivienne watched as her uncle helped escort the coffin. She had managed to keep her composure the entire day, but when she passively watched her mother be lowered into the ground, that composure dwindled. There existed five stages of grief. Denial, anger, bargaining, depression, and acceptance. As the dirt covered up the last of the wooden coffin, there was nothing left to deny. Anger exerted too much energy. So, stage three it was, bargaining.

Vivienne had decided not to have a wake and viewing. It seemed cruel to have her mother up for display. She couldn't handle the thought of people scrutinising her frail, hairless body. Sofia suggested organising a memorial service with drinks and food. Vivienne wasn't opposed at the time—it seemed like a good idea—but now she was dreading it.

The memorial was intended to be a small gathering, although somehow, the invitation had managed to find itself in the hands of a surplus of sixty people.

'I think your speech was brave.' A voice drifted from beside Vivienne. Next to her was Andrea, Marion's childhood friend that she had little knowledge about.

'Thank you . . .' Vivienne responded. 'It's Andrea, right?'

'Yes.'

'I listened to your eulogy. How is it my mother never mentioned you?'

'I'm not sure. We prioritised different things in our life, I suppose. But when I look back, I admire the road she took, especially watching you today. Your mother fell in love young and wanted a family. I just couldn't do the same.' Vivienne didn't find it hard to understand. Although her mother travelled and had a good life filled with friends, she never had true freedom. There was always someone she had to answer to, expectations as a mother and a wife.

'If you don't mind me asking, what is your field of work?'

'I am in the obscure business of art curating. I work with

clients and museums and help them set up exhibitions and make sure the art is transported safely—that sort of stuff.'

'Interesting.'

'It's a good job, allowed me to travel and see some spectacular things.' She paused, as if she had noticed Vivienne wasn't fully invested in the topic of conversation. Though Andrea had mistaken her quietness for disinterest. 'I'm sure that you have many people to talk with, so I won't keep you . . . Your mother was an amazing woman.' Andrea smiled, examined Vivienne, then walked over to a table that had a variety of different bite-sized foods. Vivienne stood there for a second, trying to orientate herself, then wandered over to a table specifically reserved for members of Marion's immediate family. She inhaled softly, allowing a cold stream of air to replenish her lungs, then placed her bag on the floor and sat in her seat. As she exhaled, the potent smell of vanilla jabbed her nostrils. For a split second, she thought she was bleeding. She turned around to locate the smell. It was such a sweet perfume for such a despicable and vile person.

'Vivienne.' The words slithered and burrowed into her ear canal.

'Grandmother.'

'My condolences for your loss.' She had a lot of nerve showing up in a place she wasn't welcomed.

'I didn't realise you were invited.'

'I wasn't. But I thought I should make an appearance. I *was* her mother-in-law, after all.' How dare she. She hated Marion with every dying breath in her body. After all, Marion harboured Louis from her evil wrath. Or in her grandmother's mind, stole him.

'What do you need?'

'I'm wondering if you have seen your father. I would like to speak with him,' she said, as her—almost—black eyes stared into Vivienne's soul.

'I'm not sure where he is. But I don't think he's interested in talking to you.'

'A birdie told me that he isn't very interested in talking to you either.' Her tone had become subtly mocking. 'I'm sure he hasn't gotten far.'

'I'll make sure to write a note to turn up to your funeral unannounced.'

Her grandmother acknowledged the snarky comment but didn't respond. Instead, she shed her skin and slid away.

'What was that about?' Thomas said, sneaking up behind her.

'Nothing. No need to worry.'

'Are you sure?'

'Yes, just leave it.'

'Alright.' Thomas looked around, as if to see if someone was watching. 'I know this isn't your scene, so say the word and we can sneak out back.'

She considered the idea. She needed to get away, escape from this place. It would have been unfair to leave Adrion, though. She couldn't just leave him alone at her mother's memorial.

'Fine. Let's go.' Or maybe she could.

Slowly, they began walking to the back of the venue, ensuring no one noticed them. As she charged through the door, she felt free from the pain the day had imposed on her.

'How about we go back to your place?' Thomas suggested.

'I think Dad will be home. but there's nothing to lose in checking.' She still couldn't face her father, not after he blatantly ignored her at the church.

It felt like old times, walking down the familiar streets. As they arrived at the house, she peered through one of the windows, trying to detect any signs of life.

'Shit.'

'What?'

'He's here,' she whispered. This was her father, not some

stranger. Recently, he felt like a stranger, though, and she was adamant to avoid an awkward encounter at all costs.

'You still got our bicycles?' Thomas asked. When he had left to live in Canada, he couldn't take his bicycle—for obvious reasons—so she kept it. She knew how much he loved it and couldn't bear the thought of it being thrown out or given away.

She sneered. 'Of course I still have them.'

'Okay, well, get to it, let's go for a ride. We can sneak around the back. Would the shed be open?'

'Yes, we never lock it.'

'Good.' Thomas walked around the side of the house, unlocked the green gate, and descended the small walkway. When he returned, he had both bicycles, one in front of him and the other trailing behind.

'It's been a while, hasn't it?' Vivienne savoured the sight. Seeing their bicycles next to each other was something she used to take for granted.

Racing down the streets with him allowed her to forget, even if it was temporarily. As the break in the clouds closed, rain began to drizzle down. Slowly, it became heavier and heavier, until the rain was beating their scalps and their vision was too compromised to go any further.

Thomas screamed at the top of his lungs, utter freedom evident on his face. Vivienne took her hands off the handlebars and dangled them in the air, embracing the rain and the cold. They looked at one another and laughed.

'Hey, isn't that old pavilion around here? The one we used to go to after school sometimes?' he said, fighting to be heard over the rain.

Vivienne peddled in front and took the lead. 'Yeah, it is. Take a left.'

As they turned into the street, they were greeted by a dainty park with an old manor. They hastily dropped their bicycles and ran through the gates towards the white pavilion.

'I'm fucking soaked.' Vivienne laughed as she squeezed the excess water from her dress, which was now less of a maroon colour and more of a brown.

'Me too.' Thomas took off his shirt and laid it on the rail of the pavilion. As Vivienne went to stand, her dress caught the heel of her shoe, and she stumbled, falling onto Thomas. There was a small thud as they hit the floor. She laughed as she pulled the hair stuck on her face. Thomas stared at her, smiling. Her laugh eventually came to a halt and the only sound left was the rain and tension between them. Her head lowered and his rose, like magnets. It was meant to stop, but his panting felt so safe. Before she knew, her cold blue lips were against his. Together, they once were a vast, burning fire, now reduced to embers. But no matter how much oxygen they pumped, there was no hope. Their fire was never intended to last. Adrion's voice infiltrated her mind, and she quickly tore her lips away.

'I can't,' she said.

'I know.' He sat up. 'I let you slip through my fingers. You and I, Vivienne, we were meant for each other. But maybe just not now. Not in this life.' The look of defeat washed over him, knowing he would never have her as a whole. Never in her entirety. A part of her would always be his, and they both knew that. 'I'm leaving Paris on Tuesday; I have to go back.' Vivienne knew she couldn't have him, but somehow, it felt as though she was losing him a second time. She felt sick. 'There's nothing here for me anymore.'

'You don't have to go.'

He looked at her, as if to tell her to stop being naïve. 'We both know that's not an option.'

She looked at him intensely. 'I'll drive you to the airport on Tuesday.'

Vivienne stepped out of Thomas's car without looking back. She desperately tried to remind herself that her future was in front of her. She rang Adrion's doorbell, her dress dripping and sticking to her legs. As he stepped out, she was overcome with guilt at the realisation that she had been unfaithful.

'You're soaked. What happened?' Adrion opened the door with a worried look.

'I got caught in the rain.'

'Where were you after the memorial? I tried finding you.'

'Thomas and I went back to my place.'

'Vivienne, you can't just run off and leave me in the dark. It's not fair.' He covered his face, frustrated.

'I'm just overwhelmed at the moment, alright?' she muttered dismissively, as she slipped off her heels.

'When are you going to realise that you're not the only person in this relationship?' A forceful tone penetrated the air.

'You don't think I know that? I know that, okay? I am on the verge of hypothermia, my mother is dead, and all you can do is stand there and interrogate me. So, if you wouldn't mind moving, that would be fucking fantastic.' She raised her voice, then barged past him. She didn't know how it was possible, but everything had become worse. Adrion was the scaffolding that prevented her from peeling apart. However, even at that moment, her mind was on Thomas, her number of precious people down by one. Her feeble heart had been left with no padding to withstand another fall.

CHAPTER TWENTY

'Here we are.' Vivienne parked the car and looked at Thomas.

'Barely. Organisation was never your strong point, Viv,' he responded impishly as he unbuckled his seatbelt and exited the car; her poor time management had once again prevailed. She hadn't seen Thomas since the day of the funeral, although she had desperately wanted to. It wouldn't have been fair for either of them. There was still an obligation she felt to honour her decision to drive him to the airport. Thomas may have been able to joke, but behind his eyes, she could tell he was suffering.

'Come back soon. Won't you?' Vivienne asked, while she helped him roll his suitcases through the airport. There was little sincerity in her comment—the utter truth was she hoped she never had to see him again.

'Paris is my home. Of course I'll come back.' She could recognise his lies. 'My plane is boarding soon. I should probably go.'

'Safe travels.' The words sounded like plastic, so forced, so fake. She sounded like a worried mother sending her child off to war. There was an army of things she wanted to say, though words wouldn't do her thoughts justice. She stared at him one last time and smiled, observing his face and cherishing every feature. Opening her heart, she desperately crammed in the last few moments with him. She turned around, as satisfied as possible, and began to leave.

Thomas grabbed the palm of her hand and drew her towards him. 'I'm sorry.' Vivienne froze, too stunned to speak. She could see through his eyes he was in anguish, and she wanted so badly to strip him of that pain. To kiss him and tell him she was his. What did he mean he was *sorry*? Sorry for what? Sorry for being too late? As she stood there alone, watching his back, she knew why he was apologising. There was a phrase Vivienne's mother used to tell her as a child. It related to books, but it felt fitting for the situation she had found herself in. Her mother used to say, 'It is impossible to rewrite history.' Vivienne had let the past take advantage of her, assault her, and leave her bloody and bruised. She had thought Thomas re-entering her life was a divine blessing, but with clear vision, she could tell it was a cruel trick. She had tried to catch an illusion, a husk of something that no longer existed. And in the process, she had let what she was holding slip through her fingers.

As she approached her car, tears as thick as blood fell down her face. She tilted her head towards the sky and watched as Thomas's plane flew overhead, until it disappeared into the clouds. She opened the door of the car and slammed it shut. With her hands, she created a tight fist and began to beat the steering wheel. The more she struck, the more fury surged through her. This was an anger she hadn't experienced for a long time, an anger so powerful that trees uprooted themselves to escape her wrath. Vivienne stepped on the accelerator of the car and sped through the streets aimlessly. She wondered what would happen if she didn't raise her foot off the pedal. What if she forgot to take it off? Sometimes, she felt attracted to death, as if it was calling for her. And ever since her mother had passed, she could feel it practically begging her. She felt tempted by the void, the serenity of it. Before this thought consumed her, she caught a glimpse of a small grocery store on the corner of a nearby street, and she had a better idea to ease the pain. Without another thought, Vivienne turned sharply to the right, swerved, and parked her car. The grocery store crouched there, on the corner of an alleyway, old and in need of maintenance. It was the type of shop that concealed something sinister, like a fugitive, or the mafia. Vivienne took a second to locate the aisle that housed the alcohol. Without hesitation, she picked up three bottles of liquor and shoved them into her bag, whatever was strongest. If she couldn't feel good, maybe it was better to feel nothing at all. She dragged herself towards the cashier, the bottles chiming beside her.

'Having a party, are we?' the man behind the counter asked as the bottles flowed out of Vivienne's bag like a poorly orchestrated magic trick.

'Party for one,' she said, watching his chubby fingers dial in the prices.

'I've been there. The world is always against you, isn't it?' The man spoke without making eye contact. She couldn't ascertain whether the comment was supposed to be comforting or rude, so she tried to ignore it.

'I'm not a drunk, if that's what you're insinuating. I just like my liquor.'

'You don't have to convince me,' the man said as he passed Vivienne her bag.

She returned to her car and drove towards her apartment, now an imprisoning haven where time stopped, or at least slowed. There was one thing in her way though: Chloe. Another interaction was the last thing she needed.

'Vivienne,' Chloe leant against the railing of the stairs and whispered.

'Hi, Chloe.' Out spat a reluctant response.

'I hate to be a pain, but could I borrow some flour?' All she wanted to do was drown her misery in peace, but now she had to cater to her neighbour's unhealthy baking addiction.

'It's no problem. Come in.' Vivienne could sense Chloe's heavy eyes fixated on the bottles of liquor that poked through the surface of her bag. 'Don't mind all the alcohol, I'm having a party.' Her quick, impulsive lie kept her from unwanted questioning.

'Nothing better.'

'Here you go. Enjoy your baking.' The bag of flour left a stained streak as it slid across the bench.

'I will. I'll make sure to bring you some,' Chloe responded as Vivienne ushered her out the door. As soon as the lock clicked, Vivienne snatched one of the bottles, sat at her desk, and unscrewed the lid. There was no need for any glasses—she didn't intend to leave remnants of the night.

Friendship, a state of mutual trust and support between two people. What was desirable in a friend? Trust, obviously. Loyalty, perhaps. Attention? Friendship was complicated, but alcohol wasn't. Alcohol couldn't betray Vivienne or share unwanted opinions. It couldn't talk back to her or make her feel culpable. It simply posed there, pretty and disinterested.

With the liquor in her stomach, she could float freely, without judgement. It may have seemed pleasurable, but liquor could only provide a shallow friendship, one with little meaning. Lying on the cold bathroom tiles, she now realised its peril. The last of her supply had diminished, and now she was experiencing the full effect of her decisions. Bonnie looked over her from above the toilet, like Lady Justice. The sobering thoughts felt disorientating, as if she had been in a coma, deprived of time. How many days had it been? Was the smell of rotting carcases coming from the kitchen or the lavatory? Vivienne wrapped her arms around the toilet and heaved herself up. One mystery had been solved. She assumed that her intoxicated self would have been courteous enough to flush and wipe the vomit that had been smeared around the seat. Eventually, Vivienne gained enough strength to stand. She picked herself off the ground and placed her feet one after the other, just as she had done as a toddler. Only this time, she was an adult with a profuse substance abuse issue. In the kitchen were multiple broken plates, an open tin of cat food situated next to Bonnie's upside-down bowl, dirt streaks along the floors and bench, and a filthy towel to accompany it all. And lastly, three half-eaten, shrivelled apples that had fallen from the bin. She may have created the mess, yet she was revolted. The desk was in less of a dire state. For a matter of fact, it was spotless, not a loose piece of paper in sight. On further inspection, there were three keys on her typewriter that had vanished. However, she distinctly remembered how they had gone missing. Placed horizontally next to the type-writer were more pages of the esteemed manuscript. When she wasn't drinking, she was writing; these were the only parts of the days she remembered. Before Vivienne had the oppor-tunity to put the clues of her depressing bender together, her throat began to burn. She swiftly closed her mouth as the vomit swished around, the liquid oozing out as she raced to the bathroom. Dropping to the floor, she knelt and spewed, her scruffy hair dangling in front of her, managing to catch the bulk of the vomit. The excess landed everywhere but the bowl. Grabbing the end of her black sweater, she pulled it over her head and wiped the lump-filled mess off herself. She drew the shower curtain to the end of the bath and twisted the faulty faucet. It slowly rose with water, as Vivienne passively watched and reflected. This wasn't how she envisaged herself; she had strayed so far from the path. Pandora's deadly, unforgiving box had been opened and she didn't know if she had the power to close it. She just wanted to fade away into nothing.

Vivienne hoisted her body over the white ceramic ledge and

into the steamy pool of bliss that spilled out the sides onto the surrounding tiles. The temptation to have another drink was calling her. She was surprised Adrion hadn't shown up at her doorstep or called either. He had finally dipped his toe into the pool of self-respect. She knew that if their relationship was going to continue, she would need to reconcile of her own volition. But one thing at a time—her priority was sobriety. Vivienne drained the bath water that had gone cold and made her way to her bedroom. Slipping into the covers was undeserved indulgence. Her head was still spinning, yet she enjoyed its nurturing rocking.

Vivienne pushed the doors of the lecture hall slightly and slithered in. She was wearing black sunglasses to hide the unpleasant state of her eyes, and her hair was cut to a shoulder-length bob, another thing drunk Vivienne decided to bless her with. However, she had to admit, she didn't mind it. Sitting in the back of the lecture hall, she placed all her outstanding assignments in front of her. She was depressed, not a monster after all, and being studious was one of Vivienne's irrefutable strengths. She didn't pay much attention to the lecture. The first reason was her debilitating hangover, and the second was that she had already studied the lesson. Due to her extended leave and mother's illness, Professor Clarke had set her up with a copy of the course outline and all the necessary resources. Usually, she would chime in because she liked the professor's valuable insight. But this day did not fall in that category.

'Professor Clarke.' Vivienne crept towards her as the rest of her peers packed and exited. Professor Clarke stood up with urgency. 'Vivienne,' she said, calmly scrambling from her desk. 'I didn't realise you were here today. I was wondering when you would appear again. I tracked down that Adrion boy you're always with and asked if he had seen you. But nothing.'

'I've been under the weather lately,' Vivienne said as she

lifted the glasses from her face. The small layer of foundation wasn't enough to cover the bulging black bags under her eyes. Her jaw and cheekbones had become more prominent, and it had made her look unwell. She was already a dainty thing, although now she looked more like a malnourished dog from a shelter.

Professor Clarke scanned her face. 'You are looking rather pale.' She paused. 'On another note, however, the publishers are getting sceptical about your existence.' Vivienne didn't want to jeopardise her opportunity, and she realised their patience would eventually run out.

'Well, I've finished the manuscript. When would they like to meet?' Professor Clarke seemed oddly relieved. It was all a façade, though—the manuscript wasn't completed, but it was close enough.

'I am so glad you've said that. How does next week, Thursday, suit?'

'I have no issues with that,' Vivienne said without hesitation.

'One more thing,' the professor interjected as Vivienne slid her glasses on and prepared to leave. 'I'm not sure what's happening at the moment, and quite frankly, it isn't my business.' She lowered her voice. 'But sobriety looks much better on you.' Was it that obvious? Vivienne was sure her excuse of being sick masked her crippled state. 'These publishers do not muck around. And your great penmanship can only take you so far.' It was a slap in the face. She didn't want Professor Clarke's image of her to be tainted. She had the utmost respect for her, and now she feared she had disappointed.

'I won't lie to you. These past few weeks have been hell— worse. But I can assure you, this means more to me than you could imagine. I will not let this opportunity pass me by,' Vivienne said earnestly. This was what she was fighting for now. The battles of her past had to remain in the past.

One of the most primitive aspects of human life was maintenance. However, maintenance was, more often than not, far from exhilarating. A large portion of it was mundane. Vivienne was realising that now. Just because she had stopped didn't mean the world stopped with her.

CHAPTER TWENTY-ONE

'Now, when you meet them, make yourself likable.' Professor Clarke paused and took a small sip of her coffee, then placed the cup onto the table. 'Have an opinion, but not too much of an opinion. They want to know that they can work with you.' Vivienne's ears perked. It sounded as if the publishers were more interested in controlling her rather than working with her. Professor Clarke had gone into extreme detail surrounding the dos and do-nots when it came to her interview process, but everything she had said had a way of contradicting itself. For instance, she had told Vivienne to act 'casual', but then only minutes later had told her to be 'professional'. She didn't know how one could combine the two—maybe it was possible, but definitely not for her. Professor Clarke had gone on to explain that these publishers were the 'pillars' of literature. Vivienne knew about Maison D'Escoffrey and knew the prestige that came with their books. That's why, when Professor Clarke revealed them as the publisher who was interested in her work, she was in disbelief. The company was very selective with what they published, and although they had been off the radar the past few years, people still respected them.

'Today, you will be meeting Lucette and Andrew. Lucette is a pleasure to work with, very understanding. Almost mother like.'

Professor Clarke wrapped her hand around the cup of coffee, took her spoon, and scraped the beige foam from its ceramic bottom. 'Andrew, on the other hand, can be a bit more difficult to work with. He's firm. His father founded Maison D'Escoffrey and entrusted it to him once he had passed. He feels the need to keep the image of the company flawless . . . A pain in the arse, if you ask me,' she subtly whispered. 'So when he hammers you with questions, don't feel personally attacked. It's just in his nature.' She was talking faster than usual. Vivienne was having difficulty retaining the information that was hurling towards her.

'We'd better be on our way. Nothing worse than if we were late.' Vivienne slipped the comment in before another round of instructions shoved their way into the conversation.

The professor nodded. 'Agreed.'

They both picked up their handbags and began the short walk to Maison D'Escoffrey, which was only a few doors down from the café they had had breakfast at. Vivienne had passed by the building before; it looked similar to most buildings in Paris, except for a few distinguishing features, like its tall, cylinder-shaped entrance that ended at the contemporary glass roof. The entrance had an arched door with a crest on the top that depicted a bear holding a sword on an inwards slant. Vivienne recognised the emblem and had seen a few books with it, lying around the bookstore.

When she entered the building, she was met with an elongated reception desk that had a woman in the centre. On each side of the room were four chairs that surrounded a low, round glass table. It was a large area that felt as if it had the purpose to intimidate the people who strolled through. Vivienne wasn't bothered by its emptiness and actually found it peaceful. Professor Clarke took a seat at one of the waiting areas and Vivienne followed. Shortly after, a man appeared from behind them. Professor Clarke stood up, Vivienne closely mimicking.

'Andrew.' She hugged him affectionately. 'I would like to introduce you to Vivienne.'

'Ah, the myth herself. Suzan holds you in such high regard. And after reading your work, I have to say, so do I.' Vivienne examined his demeanour. He seemed tough, but in such a way that was endearing. He had a heavy and slightly husky voice, which fit his rugged face perfectly.

'I'm glad to be here,' she responded.

'I'll take you up to the office. Lucette is up there waiting already.'

'Okay.' Vivienne squeezed past one of the chairs and followed Andrew. She quickly flicked her head back and looked behind her. Vivienne hoped Professor Clarke would also be in the meeting but felt reassured by her proud, motherly smile.

While ascending the flights of stairs, she managed to catch a glance of a few other rooms in the building. There were several vacant offices and the place almost felt haunted. There weren't enough people to justify all the lonesome rooms. Vivienne understood that the big building was about prestige, but it seemed like a waste.

'Hi, Vivienne.' Lucette stood up and shook her hand.

'Take a seat,' Andrew said, as Vivienne pulled out one of the chairs surrounding the wooden table that seated eight.

'Where is everyone?'

'What do you mean?'

'I mean . . .' Vivienne paused. 'All of your employees.'

Andrew laughed. 'Oh, a lunch thing.' She found it odd, but acceptable, she supposed. 'Anyways, as I'm sure you're aware, we've read your manuscript—great, by the way—and are interested in taking it and turning it into a book. But we do want to know who we're working with first of all. We need to know that you'll fit our image.'

Scepticism crawled down Vivienne's spine. This sounded

more like a cult than a publisher. Wasn't what she presented solely about the writing? Why did it matter if she fit their image? Only now had the realisation set in that she would not only be selling her book, but herself. Something about it made her feel odd, because until that moment, herself and her writing had been two different entities. She didn't think that it mattered who she was, that she could hide behind her words.

'What would you like to know?' She suddenly didn't feel like talking about the book, or herself, but she realised she had no choice now.

'Maybe who you are, and your inspiration for this story,' Lucette said, stoically.

'Well.' She thought for a second. 'Growing up, I was always surrounded by books, whether I wanted to be or not. It was imposed on me and it's one of the things I'm forever grateful for. My mother owned a bookshop in Montreuil. She recently passed away.' Vivienne didn't necessarily enjoy playing the guilt card but knew it would help her cause. 'My inspiration for this book came from many different places. As someone who some-times struggles to express their emotions, I find that writing provides solace and safety. This book and its characters depict the love and difficulties I've faced over the past couple of years. Many of the characters are based on the people in my life. And I suppose that's why they're written well.'

'And I'm curious. There's a Romeo and Juliette dynamic that is quite prevalent. But why did you choose a maid and this young, affluent man?' Andrew asked, curiously.

'I like the idea of unconventional love, and I wanted to explore power imbalance and the effect it has on people. I chose to give both the characters a voice in the story, each giving their point of view in a sequence of alternating chapters. Relationships are complex, and there are constant conflicts of interest and misunderstandings that spiral out of control.

My novel illustrates that in a more physical form,' Vivienne explained with passion. Lucette and Andrew's veiled eyes met briefly. She couldn't tell what the look meant, but they seemed to understand one another.

'Well, I loved that idea of alternating points of views. It's something that's hard to execute, but you did it in such a flawless way. There was this dramatic irony throughout the manuscript that had me almost kicking myself. But in the best way possible.' He flicked through his copy of the manuscript that was in front of him. 'You had a moment in the middle involving the brother that I loved. Well placed and well timed, and I think it sets up a nice trajectory for the ending. But the ending did throw me off guard a little bit. It took such a morbid turn. The scene with the shovel was . . . gruesome.'

'What can I say? I've never enjoyed the *happily ever after*,' Vivienne said. Andrew let out a miniscule laugh. He was undeniably impressed with her wit.

'I think the visceral imagery really captures the escalation of their hatred for each other. There are some things we'd like you to alter, just minor things, with your approval, of course, and then we can work towards the editing process and design and whatnot.' The word 'alter' made her feel doubtful, but nothing could triumph her dream of feeling the smooth, laminated book cover in her hands. 'Another thing you should note is we're a very tight-knit family, and loyalty is important to us.' There it was again, those cult undertones seeping through. 'The industry is becoming more competitive, and we need authors that want to have a relationship with us.' He took a sip of his water and wiped his lips with his forearm. 'I'll level with you, Vivienne, because I like you. In this upcoming age, things are changing, and if we don't progress with this change, we'll slowly fall behind. We want to create a new generation of authors who can propel our company forward, and I believe that you can be that for us.' Andrew stood up. 'Historically, we've been known to create "window seat books". Do you know what that means?' Vivienne didn't know exactly, but she could infer the meaning from the name.

'It means you create books that are worthy of being noticed and read,' she answered.

'Precisely. We can integrate your talent into the literary world and put you on the road to where you want to be, but all we ask in return is loyalty.' Vivienne noticed he had the tendency to ramble and repeat himself. She began to realise that Maison D'Escoffrey possibly needed her more than she needed it. What Andrew was asking for wasn't unreasonable, and she also understood that he had a company to run.

Andrew began vaguely going over the conditions of their partnership until Lucette pulled out a form from her brief-case, a contract. Vivienne's heart raced at the realisation that this was no longer a hypothetical—this was real. Everything seemed in check as her eyes continued to scan the page. Then there was an abrupt stop. Five percent—five percent of the royalties? Was that it? It seemed criminal that she had put in months upon months of hard work and would only receive a sliver of the profit. She could feel their hungry eyes glare at her. She reminded herself that money wasn't the ultimate goal and signed the contract. As the pen lifted from the page, everything felt final, secure.

'Thank you for your time. We'll be in touch. We look forward to working with you,' Andrew said as he walked her to the door. She felt fulfilled, like she had gone to a large banquet and ate her money's worth. The rows of desks and scattered sticky notes had reminded her of Hugo. She wondered how he was, what he was doing lately. Was he still grieving? She slipped her hand into her bag, pulled out a notepad, and wrote on the small, lined page, *have lunch with Hugo.*

The kettle started to whistle. Vivienne ignored it, too engrossed in the 'notes to author' that Andrew had left strewn along the script. As someone who took scrutiny to heart, she was taking the feedback with grace. She liked a few of the ideas he proposed; they added some nice flourishes. However, some were just ludicrous. He had told her he enjoyed the ending, yet he wanted to change almost every aspect of it. She had been tossing up another—alternative—ending, one that was perhaps even more unsatisfying and unconventional than the first one, but she had decided to use the first one as a safeguard. The other one was very unsavoury, she could admit. Vivienne stood from the couch and strolled to the kettle, her eyes glued to the pages of the manuscript. As she poured the misty water from the pot, a thump at the door echoed through the apartment. It didn't take a crystal ball to know who may have been knocking at that time of the night. She laid the manuscript on the kitchen bench and made her way towards the door of dread.

'Didn't expect to see you here.' She looked Adrion in the eye.

'Neither did I, if I'm being completely honest,' he said, stepping into the apartment, clearly upset. 'Do you notice how unhinged you are? And do you notice how oblivious you are to everything and everyone around you?' He crossed his arms and shrugged.

'What do you mean?'

He shook his head. 'Don't act stupid.'

What was he referring to? She wasn't acting stupid. Sure, she had fled the scene of the crime, ignored him, she knew that. But she had always done that. She needed space from his smothering. 'I'm not acting stupid.' Conviction weaved its way through her voice.

Adrion followed her into the kitchen as she continued to pour her tea. 'Were you seriously that fucked?' He raised his voice slightly, his words a foreign sound to her untuned ears.

'Adrion, I have no idea what you're talking about?' she replied, matching his tone.

'Have the past few weeks been that much of a blur? You're a drunk, Vivienne. I have seventeen missed calls from you, saying that you "love me" and "miss me" and that you "fucked up".' Did she really say that? Her memory was extremely unreliable; lying, though, would have been completely unbeneficial to him.

'What do you want me to say?'

'I'm not looking for a correct answer, Vivienne, this isn't some sick test.' He covered his face with his hands out of frustration. 'I want you to pick me with your voice, God damn it. You can't say that you love me when you're drunk and then treat me like shit when you're sober.' His voice quietened. 'I have done nothing but love you and you constantly pick everything and everyone else over me, whether it's Thomas or that fucking book. You take me for granted.'

'I don't take you for granted. I love you, Adrion. But I am suffering at the moment. I feel like I'm being chased by this abyss—' She flailed her hands forward. 'And if I don't keep running, it's going to kill me.' Her voice started to quicken and shudder. 'Do you understand?'

'I am never your priority.'

'You are the person I love, Adrion, but I have other things going on. My life doesn't revolve around you.'

'I'm not asking it to revolve around me. You are so detached from reality, so high and mighty in your lonely little ivory tower.' Vivienne could feel her chest constrict out of anger. He hadn't lost his mother, had he? Or lost a foetus of a love. He didn't have a single idea what she had endured.

'Stop, for God's sake, please. I can't deal with this, not right now.' She leant her head forwards, looking at the floorboards, trying to regain her composure. 'I need to get back to my writing.'

'And here we go again. There is always something more important.' Adrion chuckled with fury. 'Here's one for you: choose.'

A dazed look struck her. 'Excuse me?'

'Didn't I make myself clear? Pick.'

'An ultimatum. Really? Stop being fucking childish.' The nerve he had to even suggest choosing between the person she loved and her labour of love.

'To be completely honest, I think I'm the only adult here.'

'Don't make me choose,' she said softly, her white flag raised.

Adrion scoffed. 'You can't do it, can you? Fuck this,' he murmured under his frosty voice. 'There is something severely wrong with you, Vivienne, the way you treat people. Marion would be appalled by what you've become.'

'Get the fuck out. Now.' The words barely escaped her mouth. Tears had built up in her eyes, but she refused to let them fall in front of him. She stood there like poison ivy, deadly, misunderstood, and unwanted. As Adrion slammed the door behind him, Vivienne knew a crucial decision had to be made. A decision that would impact her immeasurably.

CHAPTER TWENTY-TWO

Pen to paper. It seemed that was the only thing Vivienne could do right lately. She had been defenceless against the carnage of the previous night. She, and her words, had been misconstrued. She wasn't a selfish person, and she wanted Adrion to know that. He had taken her sadness out of context and made her seem like a devil. She never wanted this, his mind to see her as this little red man with horns and a tail. She knew that a halo didn't hang from her head, but surely she wasn't the devil. Picking up her pen, she began her letter to Adrion, this time prepared. She could finally use words with intent, find the perfect ones for her without being bombarded by uncontrollable emotions.

After mere minutes, Vivienne placed down her pen, folded the letter, and positioned it inside an envelope. She got into her car and drove through the streets towards the outskirts of town. A thirteen-minute drive she was familiar with. She watched as the cream-coloured buildings turned into single standing homes, until her thirteen minutes were up, and all that that remained was the fence that separated her from him. She unlocked the gate and walked to the front door.

'Hello, Vivienne.' Sofia opened the door and looked at her with her regular, benevolent eyes.

'Sofia, hi. Could I talk to Adrion for a second?'

Sofia's attention drifted towards the staircase behind her. 'I don't know if that's such a good idea.'

'Please. It's important.' It was clear that she was only trying to protect her son, but this couldn't wait, not another second.

Sofia sighed. 'I'm sorry, Vivienne.'

'Could you at least hand this letter onto him, please?' she said, lifting her hand with the crisp white envelope.

Sofia paused as if she were contemplating rejecting the request. 'I'll make sure he gets it.'

'I hope this helps him understand. I'm not a bad person.' Behind Sofia, she could see the dining table that had nourished her for months and the stairs that ran to the heart of the house, the reason she was there. It hurt her that she was now cast out from a place almost called home. She couldn't see the barrier that prevented her from entering, but it was there, like an electric fence, humming. Her love for something—or someone—always seemed to multiply the moment it was out of reach. *Everything good must come to an end*, but that wasn't really true—self-destruction was just human nature. She could have been in bed, listening to their spotless vinyls, holding his sweet head. Vivienne walked towards the gate, wondering if she'd ever come back to this place.

'Wait.' Sofia called out and lifted her dress, just enough to allow her feet to move freely, and scurried towards Vivienne.

'Yes?' she replied.

'I want you to know that I don't think you're a bad person. Adrion has told me his side of the story. Well, yelled his side of the story. However, I know that there are always two sides to every story. No mother wants to see their child in so much pain, but what I want to say is that you're not the villain. There is rarely a villain when it comes to love.' Sofia reached for Vivienne's hands, held them waist high, and lowered her voice.

'Love goes through many phases and changes. Adrion loves you, and by the looks of it, you love him too. You wouldn't be standing here otherwise.' She paused. 'But sometimes, love isn't enough. My advice to you, Vivienne, is focus on yourself for a while. We can only love someone as much as we love ourselves. And it is important to build a beautiful garden before wanting butterflies.' She released her hands, allowing them to drop and bounce off her thighs.

Vivienne watched from afar as Sofia closed the front door. It was at that moment the realisation set in that there was somebody she had treated worse than Adrion. She had neglected herself, tried to find cheap thrills and distractions, but if everything that kept her together was stripped away, she didn't know if there would be anything left of her. Anything of substance. If left alone with nothing, would the company of her own mind have been enough? Sofia was right—how could she possibly maintain a meaningful relationship with Adrion when she couldn't even have one with herself? She had been using the things and people around her as a compass. She had let Thomas and the book and the publishers lead her astray. Was her dream worth this, the pain? Could some pages keep her whole and bound? Was her destiny to become some lonely, middle-aged woman who dedicated her life to her career, with only some stupid books to insulate the raging hole in her heart? Anxiety consumed her. She wished more than anything that she could've turned to someone, but no one wanted to have anything to do with her. Not Thomas or her father, and definitely not Adrion. The only person who didn't loathe her existence was six feet underground. Which reminded her, she hadn't seen her mother since the funeral.

The ignition of her car spat as she twisted the key. After driving to a nearby flower shop and picking a bouquet of carnations, she made the unfamiliar journey to the cemetery. It was an old cemetery, tall, century-old trees casting a gloom over the place. Many of the gravestones were overrun with weeds and vines. Some of the plaques were barely visible from the rust and weathering. It didn't matter though, because at that point, those people were long forgotten, a relic of the past no one cared for. She took a short walk down the vaguely established rows and arrived at the family plot. There everyone was: her great grandparents, her grandparents, and now her mother. Next to Marion was an empty plot for her father. They intended to grow old and die together, but how was the cancer supposed to know that? Vivienne placed the flowers at the forefront of her mother's grave, then sat and wrapped her arms around her knees. The dirt was still fresh from the day she had been buried, with the exception of a few patches of grass that had sprouted.

'Hey, Mama.' Vivienne began to speak, her head faced away from the grave. 'Professor Clarke at the university helped me get my book signed with a group of publishers. She's really had my back these past couple of months.' Vivienne quivered. 'I'm afraid I don't have much other good news to tell you,' she said, smearing her watery eyes and nose with the sleeve of her top. 'Dad still won't talk to me. I'm hoping he comes around eventually.' The tremors in her voice were more prevalent now. 'Thomas left to go back to Canada. He was at the funeral. He read a nice eulogy, in typical Thomas fashion. Adrion and I aren't on speaking terms right now, and I know I only have myself to blame, but it still hurts.' She paused as someone walked past. She was sure many people talked to their loved ones, but nonetheless, she feared being judged. 'I don't know, I never thought you would die. I guess, in my mind, you were immortal.'

Vivienne stood up from the ground and looked at her mother's gravestone. 'In loving memory of Marion'. That's all she was now, a memory. She knew her mother wasn't there because she couldn't feel her soul. Staring at that cold, lifeless, polished stone confirmed her scepticism; there was no God. No God could justify stealing her mother away and making her suffer. She took comfort in knowing that if her mother's soul was out there, though, it wouldn't have been lingering in a place like this. Vivienne had tried to wrap her head around the idea of death time after time, and the finality of it all. How could something living with intelligence and emotion simply wither away into nothing? How could eternal darkness be the end of the journey? Life was the ultimate effort in vain.

Vivienne arrived home to her lonely, high-ceiling apartment. She had worked so hard for her independence, and that was all she was now: her independence. She opened the cabinet above the counter and took a glass and a bottle of wine.

'Fuck it,' she murmured under her breath. The contract with the publishers had been signed and secured, and sobriety was overrated. She sat on her thin balcony and allowed for the liquid to warm her throat. She had never experienced solitude like this before, but there was something almost comforting about it. She had hit rock bottom, and the only option was to either soak in its dim misery or make the slow, rickety ascent back to the top.

CHAPTER
TWENTY-THREE

Vivienne's fingertips slowly slid over the spines of the books. 'S. Clarke,' she muttered continuously. Then her fingers stopped in their tracks. She took a book from the shelf and looked at the cover. Her beloved professor's black and white face boldly stared back at her, with three large, navy-blue words that went vertically down the page: *'All unpredictable odds.'*

'Just this one, please,' Vivienne said, placing it down on the front desk of the library.

The librarian flipped the book over and inspected it.

'Very interesting read,' she said as she stamped the back. 'Autobiographies can sometimes be difficult to get through, however, this one was fascinating, very fascinating. Suzan has done so much for women in the industry.' She handed Vivienne the book. 'And from a humble beginning as well, mind you,' she added.

'Yeah, she's my professor. Thought I should know who I'm dealing with,' Vivienne joked. However, in truth, that *was* the reason she was borrowing the professor's critically acclaimed autobiography. There was a comment she had made a while back that had intrigued Vivienne, something regarding her adoptive mother, but even before the comment, it interested her who Professor Clarke actually was. There was something in the way she carried herself that was mesmerising. This ability to float on a cloud of knowledge whilst also being simultaneously grounded and understanding. Vivienne had only scratched her refined surface, but after all the attention she had received, her curiosity was sparked.

After arriving at her apartment that afternoon, she tossed herself onto the worn leather couch and sank into the fabric until it practically consumed her. She admired the cover one last time before slowly lifting it, as if its contents were about to burst out.

'*To the people who gave me a future, my mother and William*', the second page read. Vivienne flicked past the table of contents to uncover the first chapter. As she began to read, the lines uplifted themselves and danced off the page. She could see everything so clearly.

'I was abandoned on a few occasions throughout my life, left with nothing but my sanity and new beginnings. However, this was the first instance. When I was still young and naïve, it baffled me how a mother's maternal instinct could have allowed her to leave a child with nothing. Now, at my rather ripe age, my resentment has calmed, yet the question still haunts me. I was left orphaned at the age of two. Or was it three? Well, that was my first predicament. When I was found by the sisters, all I had was a piece of paper that had been tucked into the front pocket of my top. On that piece of paper was my name and nothing else. Although, one positive was that I could celebrate my birthday whenever I pleased. As comical as it may sound now, young Suzan would have begged to differ. Over the five years I spent at the orphanage, there is very little I can remember. I used to think it was because of my age and how young I was, but it was something else, a response to the trauma, to the monotony of that awful place. To the children who were taken out of bed at night and never seen again. To the lack of funding that made my stomach growl. To the "homes to be" that waltzed through those wrought-iron doors, and to the disappointment of never being picked...'

'Life was difficult, but not impossible. As someone whose life revolves around articulating and stringing words into something that leaves an impression on people, I may be biased, but if I had to refine the reason I am here today to one key thing, it would be words. From a young age, I was gifted with language. My teachers knew it, but only one helped me nurture it. Her name was Audrey Fike. She taught me that words had a profound impact, and that the right words could be the difference between achieving everything one wanted and withering away into mediocrity. I had so much to say, but without this gift of articulation, it would have been pointless. I questioned why someone like her, so cultivated and intelligent, worked in a place like that, and she told me it was because she knew she would meet someone like me. Eventually, she left and carried on. After all, there was only so much she could endure. The sisters didn't like her, and by this point, they didn't like me either. I was a poppy that was growing taller by the day, but all they wanted to do was cut me down, prune me so I was reliant on them for my very survival. I refused to let them...'

'I think I was eight at the time. The sun was gleaming, and I was in my safe place, an unattended classroom with a chalkboard. I was doing one of my favourite activities, which involved writing a word in the centre of the board and placing other similar words on a spectrum titled *negative* and *positive*. There was something enjoyable about discovering what different words meant to me and what emotions they evoked. It was like north on a compass in a world I often found myself disorientated by. I invited a few of my peers to play once, but unfortunately, it didn't catch on as I would've hoped. However, this day, I could feel a pair of eyes nurturing my side, and as I looked over, there was a woman. She approached me and told me her name was Nancy. What a beautiful name, I thought to myself. She asked me, in a sort of interrogational style, what I was writing on the board. I told her, and afterwards, she crouched down, grabbing my feeble hands, and asked, "How would you like to come and live with me?" She was like sweet simplicity, like warm bread with honey. She was like an angel sent to take me away from that place, a place I never belonged. Her husband, William, was also there, who I found out later never wanted me. They were there to adopt an heir, but Nancy and her infertility won that battle. The next day, I woke up in a generous, double-sized bed with a view of the coast and a manor to roam free in...'

'William was a high-ranking officer in the military, a vault of a man, but with the right combination, he could crack. Mother and I were the right combination. I could see through his eyes, usually when he came home from work, that he felt safe with us, that we gave him a reason to come home. I never called him my father because I never saw him as a father. Just like he was an officer in the military, he was the captain of the house. It was the turn of the decade, and we were comfortable by the coast, though fate had different plans for the three of us. One night at dinner, we received a phone call from one of William's superiors, which was never a good sign. Within a few weeks, my safe haven of three years was gone and not only were we leaving the house, but we were also leaving England for good. I read about the war that had erupted in greater Europe, but I never thought my family would have been uprooted and moved to another country. When we arrived at Abbeville, I was merely a girl, but at my eventual departure, I was a woman. The house was a bit further from town, similar to our home in England.

In fact, there were many similarities. My mother loved the house with her entire heart. She cleaned it excessively, not out of obligation but out of sheer pleasure. We did many activities together, baking and reading, and we would go into town almost every day. I was at that rare age where I was capable, yet the world expected so little from me. Sometimes, I wish I could go back. What I loved the most, however, was learning the French language. The prospect of new words excited me, this opportunity to expand my knowledge. The language frustrated my mother, but I badgered her to the brink of insanity to at least try. It was the last thing she wanted to do on this Earth, and the last thing she ever thanked me for...'

'William came and went for different periods at a time—weeks, months even. Abbeville was massacred months prior, and the town was trying its hardest to pick up the pieces. My mother and I came home from town one day and then it hit us, like an arrow with no exit wound. Through writing the accounts of my life, I have found it incredibly hard to recount some of the events, though this was by far the hardest. All I remember were two men, my mother on the floor, and the words that came from their mouths: "William was a great man who served this country well." After that, life wasn't the same for a while. My mother went into hibernation, and I tried to help her, but that big, black, ugly dog was wrapped tight around her, weighing her down...'

'I remember the day we won. It was the day Mother decided to sell the house and move to Paris. This sudden shift occurred, as if she realised that her husband was never coming back and that she needed to find a new purpose...'

'I was at the end of my schooling when we disembarked in Paris. Young, free, well-mannered, and educated, it felt though the world was my oyster. There were many things that I was passionate about, especially one cause in particular: feminism.

It took me a while to catch onto the issue that our society faced. It first struck me when I stepped into university on my first day—men as far as the eye could see. In my class of forty-six, there were three other girls besides myself. One later dropped out because of what I assumed was an unplanned pregnancy. There was this cultural issue that stuck out like a sore thumb and later became the focal point of my career...'

'I was aristocratic and knowledgeable leaving university. With a degree in French literature and sociology, I thought that finding respected work would have been easy. I was mistaken. All my male counterparts were receiving jobs out of the wood-work. So, what made me so different? The answer to that question had to remain dormant for a while longer...'

'I found my mother collapsed on the floor one evening. Two weeks later, they were tossing dirt over the coffin she laid in. It happened suddenly, just like William's death, and there was little closure. I was grateful, though, that at least this time, there was a body to bury. The doctors deemed it cancer out of incompetence. She may not have been my biological mother, but she was more than that careless silhouette of a woman could have ever been...'

'Finally, opportunity struck, and funnily enough, it found me. His name was Daniel, an old friend of my father's from back in England. I ran into him one day out of pure chance, and he talked up a storm. Then, somehow, we fell on the topic of university, where I explained my qualifications as well as my unfortunate quest for work. Without hesitation or questioning, he asked me to come work for him, and I told him yes. I knew that he worked as a journalist for one of the biggest newspapers in Paris, but it turned out that after fifteen painstaking years, he was practically running the place. He told me that he could have used someone like me on the team, which didn't make sense initially, but as I walked through those gigantic office doors, it did...'

'Some of the people at work didn't appreciate my presence. I liked to think it was because they felt threatened, but I would only have been fooling myself. I was a columnist at work, I ran an opinion column, and some of the topics I wrote about stirred up quite the controversy. I explored many issues surrounding equality and I dug deep into the systemic problem this country was facing on the issue of women's rights. My research included intimate meetings with activist groups at the time, as well as university professors who wanted to have their say on why I was "ludicrous", even challenging my own employers on the lack of female representation. They threatened to fire me at one point for defamation after I wrote a piece about the discrimination that women faced in the media industry. I count my blessing that I had Daniel. He was one of the good ones, always towing me out of the inescapable mud I found myself in...'

'I was going about my usual business, like I had been for the past three years. I was comfortable working with the company. They needed me not because they necessarily agreed with my columns, but because I made sales skyrocket. We had a saying whilst I was there, *"Any publicity is good publicity"*, and I was certainly a way to flush any competitors out. When I arrived that morning, I was greeted by an envelope on my desk with a wax seal that had an emblem of a bear. I will never forget that day. It was the day that my grit, stubbornness, and determination paid off. Although I no longer have the letter, I remember lucidly what it read.

> *'"Dear Suzan Clarke, I write you this letter with your column beside me. For a matter of fact, two of your columns. The murder of Mary Conte—brave of you to speak out on such a topic. I have booked you in to meet me at noon today. – Arthur Escoffrey."*

'I had heard about Arthur Escoffrey at the time, but my knowledge was flawed, and assumption is a dangerous thing.

Rumour had it that he was strange. Alternative, some said, which worked in my eventual favour. There was one thing that was for certain: he was wealthy, and with wealth always came power. When I arrived for my meeting, I was greeted by a young man. He looked boisterous and rough, but when he reached out to shake my hand, I knew it was a front, because his hands were as soft and gentle as warm butter. His name was Andrew. When he shone his smile, something casted upon me, and it was something that I never found again. I know that when he reads this book, he will scorn my words, but he was my Achilles heel...'

'When I was escorted to Arthur, I was greeted by everything I expected: a mysterious man who reeked of affluence and potential opportunity. He sat me down and explained that he wanted to give a voice to people who had something valuable to say but couldn't shout loudly enough. He wanted to pluck individuals out and make them pillars of society. He told me that he, and his company, aimed to be a staple of literature. And here we stand, thirty years later, relishing in his vision. He took my columns from the years I worked at the news firm, as well as articles that never made it to print, and orchestrated a book. *The Uneven Playing Field* was its title, and within two years, four hundred thousand copies had been sold and distributed around France. I was officially on the map, and so were Arthur and his company, Maison D'Escoffrey...'

'After a while, more was expected from me. Arthur took me to events where he used my success to expand his business and I used his status to build stronger connections. I wrote many books while I was with Arthur, but my most famous work was a fictional adaptation of my life as an orphan, which won French Literary Fiction of the Year. Arthur died of a stroke in the late nineteen sixties, and afterwards, Andrew took over the company, and I was his partner for a while. People used to say that love and work couldn't mix, and ultimately, they were right...'

'I had recently reached forty, and what a troublesome few years they were. It was the first instance that I realised my work and success weren't enough. The maternal instinct that I had desperately tried to suppress came flooding back. The reason I suppressed it was because I loathed it; I didn't want it to stump my progression through life. I tried to prove the people who doubted me wrong and give a voice to those who couldn't speak. I intended to set a trail of breadcrumbs so that a strong stone road could follow. However, through it all, I never questioned what I really desired, and of course, I was too late...'

'I decided to foster children, give them the same opportunity that was given to me, even if it was temporary. It satisfied that maternal instinct I have jaded you with. Some of the children were troubled. It made me wonder how my life would have turned out if I were never adopted, if I never had Nancy and William. The system had damaged these kids, and some I could help, but some refused. They only stayed for a few months at a time, many eventually finding permanent homes. One of them slapped me—her name was Leila. So fiery and passionate, only it was misdirected. The week after that incident, I adopted her. She was extremely intelligent for a fifteen-year-old, matured fast, but I suppose you have to in that environment. Three years later, she went to college, following in my footsteps. We even co-wrote a book together about her struggles in the foster system. Although I was her legal guardian, I never saw her as my daughter. She was the equivalent to a younger sister. Because I and every child I fostered were connected by one defining fact. We were all abandoned at some point, and that's stronger than any blood...'

'Recently, I was offered a job at the university I studied at. It's oddly amusing to me how there was a time I never thought a woman would step into that place with the intention to teach. Yet here we are. My hair is now starting to grey, and although my life may not be over, I felt that it was time to write this. I have lived true to who I am, and if I had to leave one piece of advice here, on this ink-riddled page, I would say that silence is easy, and the truth comes with a cost. However, the cost of regret is greater.

Suzan Clarke –

CHAPTER
TWENTY-FOUR

Winter had come around again, no harsher than the last. Vivienne opened the door to the bookstore, and the faint sound of a bell, indicating a customer, rang through the shop. Although she was no customer, she had heard that bell ring hundreds if not thousands of times when she was younger.

'It's looking good,' Vivienne said.

Louis gazed down from the ladder he was carefully balanced on. A few months after Marion had passed, he decided to try and restore the family bookstore to its former glory. It was an outlet, a way to channel the array of emotions he didn't under-stand. He was an architect, so that's what he did best. Repairing the building helped slowly heal him. Vivienne just hoped that it wasn't a temporary solution and that he would ultimately find peace by the time all its faults were fixed. When she would come and visit unannounced, she would often hear him talking to himself. When she listened carefully to what he was saying, though, she realised he wasn't talking to himself but Marion.

'It still needs some work, but it's getting there,' he responded and continued sanding the thick wooden beam. 'How's the job going?' Vivienne didn't mind the place she worked, but she was nothing special, the bottom of the food chain. She was a receptionist for some mediocre law firm only a few blocks from her apartment. The people were nice, most of them from the same family, so naturally, they took her on as their own. They invited her everywhere, and she never turned them down either. It was nice to feel part of something, even if it was temporary. It also gave her an excuse to dress up, which was an opportunity that she could rarely resist. It was only intended to pay her bills, but she had learnt to find joy in the small talk and phone calls. Her book was only days away from reaching print. Then, it was off to the bookstores, on the shelf, and—if everything went according to plan—in the hands of people all around Paris. There were royalties to be earnt as well. Andrew had given her an approximation of the figures and they weren't to be sneezed at. Once her novel was out there, she could finally weasel back into the industry and put everything in the past. She wanted to be somewhere where she could earn respect and prestige, to feel again.

'The job is good, but it's just the same old same old.' Vivienne walked down the first aisle of books and leisurely examined them. 'They're hosting a Christmas party.'

'Another one?' Louis turned around and joked.

Vivienne chuckled. 'Yes, another one. This one's smaller though, just the people from the firm and their partners.' Which was precisely the reason she was contemplating not going. Six months and six days ago, that's how long it had been since Sofia handed Adrion that letter on behalf of Vivienne, and nothing. Sofia had told her to give him time, but she didn't realise what that really entailed. She had tried to move on, but her loyalty was strictly with him, which she learnt the hard way. A month prior, she had decided to go on a date with one of the litigation attorneys' sons, Julian. The attorney had asked her if she was single. At first, she was afraid he was going to ask her out himself, but it didn't end up taking that path. Instead, he explained that his son Julian would've been perfect for her—which couldn't have been further from the truth. He was decent in the looks department, but unfortunately, that's where his luck ended. The date became so awkward at one stage that Vivienne had to make an excuse and leave. Somehow, though, the attorney's son thought the date went successfully and asked his father to see when she was available next. She charmed herself out of it, however, with a range of awkward laughs. When she arrived at the most recent of the firm's parties, Julian had someone by his side, so she assumed there were no hard feelings. She had had a brief conversation with the woman—duds always managed to find other duds, it seemed. Vivienne thought she could drown out the thought of Adrion by replacing him, but no one could replace him.

He may have tried to avoid seeing or speaking to her, but she knew he was secretly watching. Observing from afar. In her history lectures, she could feel his taciturn eyes looking at her—she had caught him a few times, even—and only days ago, his car slowly slid past her apartment block. It was clearly intentional, and she wondered to herself whether he had done this before. She knew he hadn't moved on because his eyes were fixated on her, but he was starved and wounded and surely not desperate enough to run back to her.

'It's coming to the end of the year. Do you have any plans?' Vivienne asked. Louis climbed down from the ladder and dusted the wood shavings off himself.

'I was thinking we have your cousins and aunts over. Keep our tradition going in your mother's honour.'

'I like that idea.'

'Good.' Louis shone his rare, toothed smile, then climbed the ladder to the top. 'And how's the book going?'

'It's going to print in a few days.'

A long journey of scrutiny, editing, negotiating, and more scrutiny. Andrew had been a pain in the arse, but she had grown to love him. Professor Clarke was right—he was tough to work with, but Vivienne could see he respected her balance of rigidity and flexibility. So, in the end, they gelled nicely, mostly.

'Well, when it's out, I'll have a spot for it right by the window,' he said, pointing to the front.

'I appreciate it.' Vivienne took one of the books from the shelves, went behind the counter, and placed some money in the till. 'Have you gone to see Mama this week?' She stood by the door and pushed the book into her bag.

'I was planning to go later today.'

'Okay. I replaced the flowers already last night. Thought I'd save you the trouble,' Vivienne said as she swung the door open. 'I'll come by later in the week.'

'Sounds good, Vivienne,' Louis said softly, without taking his eyes off the wooden beam that he was entirely immersed in.

It was far from perfect, her relationship with her father, but at least there was a relationship. After Marion had passed, she wasn't sure he would ever speak to her again. The words he said the night of her death still played in her mind like a broken record—*'I can't forgive you for this.'* It was ambiguous whether he said it out of anger for missing Marion's death or whether he meant it. Had he managed to stretch the walls of his heart wide enough to forgive her, or was this just acceptance wrapped in a cheap knock-off version of forgiveness? There was no way to tell with him; he was a person who—much like herself—hid everything deep within their being.

The weather started to worsen. Vivienne had heard on the radio there was a chance of flash flooding, which was extremely exciting. It was an excuse to do nothing, a free pass to ignore the world around her. Chloe, her next-door neighbour, had decided to move out of the apartment adjacent hers. It was less than ideal. Chloe was quiet enough, looked after Bonnie, and gifted her free, baked desserts. Everything anyone could've ever wanted in a neighbour. On top of it all, Vivienne was left with a priceless number of rolling pins, bowls, and cookie cutters that she didn't need, but would try to put to good use, in Chloe's honour.

As she opened the door to her apartment, a mustard-coloured envelope laid flat and fervent on the parquetry floorboards. Vivienne strolled to her desk and checked it for a name. However, there was none. Without hesitation, she slipped her thumb into the small gap on the side of the envelope and tore it open. Who was this letter from? Was it Adrion? After all this time, had he decided to write back? And if so, was it a letter of reinstatement? *'Dear Vivienne, I'm still in love with you. I'll take you back.'* Oh, how she was a dreamer. She took the letter out of its fine casing and slowly unfolded it. Her eyes skipped straight to the bottom of the page. No Adrion, instead, another name, more unexpected. Vivienne's eyes sprinted back to the top of the page.

> *Dear Vivienne,*
>
> *I hope you and your family are well. I have missed having you by my side. I know we didn't exactly leave our friendship on the most positive terms, but thank you for being there at my lowest. I know you must have many questions and I am so sorry it has taken me this long to write to you. I would like to say that you shouldn't feel any guilt for my decision to leave. This was something I needed to do for myself. The night before I left, at your apartment, I had the opportunity to reflect on my life. Growing up, I lived a sheltered life, a privileged life, but as I looked from my place of privilege, I started to realise that I didn't know who I was. I could no longer continue living in a body that*

I barely knew. I still feel lost, but it's a different type. At least now I am lost on my own accord, and I can say I'm living authentically.

Lyon is treating me well, and I'm enjoying my time at university (although I do miss sitting beside you). I also decided to dip my toe in and study philosophy, finally. Definitely something you would be into. I hope for nothing but the best for you, Vivienne, and I know we will cross paths again. Feel free to write, I'll be waiting.

PS: Don't be afraid to take the Bugatti out for a spin—I don't want it getting lonely. Plus, no one looks sexier than you driving it.

Amelie Chevalier –

Vivienne placed down the letter and leant back in her chair. She was lost for words, her mind blank. After all this time, she finally had closure. She contemplated the idea of writing back to her, then and there, but what would she have said? *'Dear Amelie, my mother's dead, Adrion left me, and when you ran off, it was the beginning of the worst months of my life.'*

As much as she loved and believed in the power of the pen, the written words wouldn't do justice to how her life had been. Vivienne knew Amelie would be back eventually. Maybe if she didn't respond, it would have given her an incentive to return. She read the letter one last time, then opened her drawer, lifted a pile of folders, and left the letter there, allowing the clutter to suppress any feelings she had. Vivienne had thought about running away after her mother's death. Everyone else had in some form or another, why hadn't she? She stood there like a statue, unwavering, letting the world shit on her. As the drawer closed, a stapled piece of paper became lodged at the back. She rummaged to find it, then once her hand gripped the edge, she tugged it out. She read the first few lines. Suddenly, her legs were up, her chair screeching and falling behind her. The coat dangled from her arm as she sped down the stairs. The car door unlocked and Vivienne sparked the ignition, her head veiled by the wet coat. Amelie's letter may have conjured an array of emotions she didn't yet understand, but there was one word that had sparked something tangible. *'Authentically'*. The sheet that Vivienne held firmly in her hand, as she steered her car through the pouring rain, was the ending. Well, an alternate ending. Through the publishing process, there was a great debate on two possible endings that Vivienne had written. She liked one, Andrew liked one. It didn't take science to determine that they didn't have their eyes set on the same ending. However, after much disapproval, Vivienne caved. But now, she wouldn't. She walked through the lobby of the publisher dripping in rain and darted directly to Andrew's office.

'Vivienne?' Lucette called from the office opposite his. 'You're soaking wet. What are you doing here?'

'I need to talk to Andrew.'

A huff shot out as he unlocked his door and appeared behind her. 'I'm right here.' His gruff voice sank into her stomach.

She walked into his office, ignoring him. 'We need to talk.'

'About what?'

'About the ending of the book.' Andrew walked around his desk and took a seat in his leather chair.

'What about the ending?'

'The fact that you denied me from having the ending that I wanted.' Her voice filled with hostility.

'Vivienne, we've been over this, we're not doing that ending,' he responded. 'It just won't sell.' Every word spilled out with emphasis.

'Don't play that card. Anything you put on the shelves will sell.' She scoffed. 'You could publish pornography and people would still buy it. I can't look back on this book and regret the ending. This is my labour of love, and I won't let you taint it.'

His face eased briefly, almost as if he were considering the idea. 'The book goes to print in less than three days.'

'We won't be going to print if this isn't the ending,' she said.

'You signed a contract, Vivienne.'

'Andrew, just listen to me. I may have written both these endings, but only one is the *true* ending. It stayed in my drawer, then I brought it to you, where you later rejected it and preferred that we edited the original ending. Then back in the drawer it went. Until I saw it today, crumpled.' Her hands imitated the events of the narration. 'It's raw and written in a dark place. And I don't know if I will ever be in such a dark place again.' She sighed with frustration. 'Please. If anything, go out on a limb for me.'

Andrew bent over the desk and snatched the paper off Vivienne. He read the first few lines and nodded his head slightly. 'It wouldn't hurt to reconsider,' he said softly. She had done it, overpowered him with sheer, untamed emotion and brute force. 'I'll look back over it this afternoon and call you tonight with a verdict.'

Vivienne stood from her chair. 'Thank you, Andrew.'

'I can't deny that you have a point. I've been playing it safe since my father passed, trying to preserve this company's image. But our image *is* our uniqueness,' he said as he broke eye contact with her and began reading the paper she had given him. 'And there is no denying that you are unique. You are powerful, Vivienne. I'm glad you know when to cut the shit and say it how it is.' She had worked with him for months and the closest they had come to an agreement was compromise, but something had sparked in Andrew's mind that instant. Maybe he realised that she was the future, a rare phenomenon. And maybe he wanted to be on the right side of her, Vivienne LaRue.

CHAPTER TWENTY-FIVE

'I'll have a cherry Danish.' Vivienne said, opening her wallet.

'Anything else, darling?'

'No, I'm all good.' Vivienne sat down on one of the chairs inside the café. It was rarely busy at this time, and most people who wandered through were considered regulars. Her usual order was a Danish or croissant, though every few months—when she was feeling adventurous—she would order a coffee from Rene's. And without failure, it tasted like dirt. She thought that someone would have given some honest feedback by that point, but even after two years, it was the same story.

'You're in an awfully good mood today. What's happened?' Rene slipped the Danish into a brown paper bag, twisted the top, and put it on the counter. They were barely on a first-name basis—despite this, casual conversation drifted through the air occasionally. Especially when Vivienne smiled or looked as though she had something to say.

'Nothing really, just going out to buy some books—a book.' She walked over and took the brown bag.

'Must be a pretty impressive book if it has you smiling like that.'

'It is.' Vivienne smiled and exited Rene's patisserie. She took the pastry out of the paper bag and used it as a sleeve. Andrew's verdict came back, and just as Vivienne suspected, he made an *executive* decision to change the ending. Days later, it went to print, and two weeks after, an initial fifteen thousand copies were distributed to bookstores around Paris, waiting to be consumed. Andrew had told her that she would receive attention from people and that she should prepare herself. That she would get the recognition she deserved. Funnily enough, he was right, and she had. Within a week of it adorning the shelves, book critics had started writing a variety of reviews. Some called her and her writing vulgar, but many thought her work was honest and a stroke of genius. There was a journalist who was writing a piece on *'modern-day young female authors'*, who asked if she would be willing to have an interview. It was out of left field, but she didn't decline. Then a few days after, there was a copy of the article at her door. She flicked through and there she was on page thirteen. *'Feminine Future'* was the title above her head, even though nearly every page prior to hers was dedicated to the success of male authors.

The publisher also received a sudden spike in interest, and any decline in popularity they were previously experiencing was no longer the case. They had authors approaching out of the woodwork in light of Vivienne's novel. She was their new talent, and it seemed many authors wanted in. As she roamed the street, she looked at the front window of every bookstore she walked past, and without fail, her novel stared back at her. When she first went to buy her book, it took her a few moments to adjust, but now, weeks later, she had acclimatised. Could this become her new norm? Her name was finally on the map. She had climbed onto the stage and now she could work her way to the top, let the spotlight soak and burn her fair skin. Vivienne stepped to the side of the pavement and entered one of the bookshops off the main plaza near her apartment. The previous night, there had been an accident involving her hand, a cup of tea, and her book. The ink had seeped through the pages, rendering it useless. So, there she was, for the second time, entering a bookstore and buying her book. She picked one from the eight that were left and ran her fingers along the hard cover. She flicked through the pages, ensuring that it was the exact same as her previous copy.

'Can I help you?' an oddly cheerful shopkeeper asked from behind her.

'No, I'm just browsing.'

'Well, you've managed to pick up a good one.' The woman inched closer to Vivienne. 'We got this in a few weeks ago. I only just finished reading it, but I honestly couldn't put it down. She's a new author, "Vivienne", but I expect we'll see more of her soon.'

'And what's the book about?' Vivienne asked. She was intrigued how the woman would explain it.

'It follows the story of this maid who caters for an absurdly rich family, and she falls in love with one of the sons. Okay, maybe more than one of them, but I don't want to spoil anything. It was a bit graphic, but if you're interested in love, tragedy, and manipulative characters, this is for you.' Vivienne nodded. She couldn't fault the brief explanation.

'Sounds like a must read. I'll get it.'

'Wonderful,' the woman responded with the same cheery tone as she had been using throughout their encounter. Vivienne couldn't tell if she was putting it on for customer satisfaction or whether she was a genuinely happy person. She pulled out her wallet and handed the lady a few notes. As she took the money, she paid Vivienne a strange look. 'Vivienne LaRue?' she whispered. Vivienne followed the lady's eyes that were squinting at her wallet. She flipped it over and looked inside. Her driver's licence was sticking out.

'I've been caught,' Vivienne joked.

'Oh my God, it is you. Your book was amazing, I was in complete awe of it. You write so beautifully, by the way. I wish I could write like that,' the woman said, now without the fake cheery tone.

'Thank you.'

The lady spun the newly bought book around and flipped over the pages. 'Since you're here, I have a question, just one. What was the meaning behind this?' She twisted it back towards Vivienne.

'How long do you have?' Vivienne paused and smiled. 'I sacrificed a lot to be here, and I never want to forget that.' Without another word, she picked up the novel and left. She flicked the cover over and gripped the first page with the tip of her index finger. What she had sacrificed to be there was unimaginable. Life had tested her, and she questioned if she had made the right choice. Life had left her out in the cold with nothing but words and ink. Although her fingers and her heart felt numb, she persisted.

Her dream cost her, not in a tangible way, but in something more. In valuable minutes, in the chance for redemption.

'To myself and those I have lost along the way', the dedication read on the second page. She had something to show now in a life that changed like the tide. Growing hurt, as the skin stretched and shed. Some days, all she wanted was to be young again. Young enough to fit wholly in her mother's arms. Young enough that her mother still existed. Her name may have meant alive, yet her name was a fantasy, something unattainable. She desperately clung onto whatever debris of joy she could find. She was only trying to survive, and maybe that had to suffice.

White dress

I look at your beautiful little waist, curving like vines. The way you dance is mesmerising. I observe your sensuality, not knowing if I want to feel you or be you. You precious thing, wipe those precious tears. You cry and cry with your watercolour eyes, radiant green, simply breath taking, begging for something more. I dream of you on the side of a hill, tall grass embracing your perfect body, watching chemtrails from the distance. You take your shoes off to feel something real—the fabric constrained you and made you sad. You long for a life where things were taken at face value. Hands on your body, bread in the oven, and daffodils that sway with the wind. A new bouquet of flowers each week is not enough to appease your lust for life. You need nature entrenched inside you. The clothes you wear start to tighten and constrict your chest, although you have been wearing them since the morning, and they had fit amply. You take off your dress and lie down, the grass now cradling you. The chemtrails start to dissipate and you hear your name in the distance. A lover, perhaps? You run, your breasts free. He kisses them tenderly like he has kissed your body thousands of times before. You can't remember where you placed your clothes, but it doesn't matter. Tears flood your eyes, hoping someone touches your body like this when your waist is no longer as small and your bones are brittle. But you find comfort in knowing that if human hands won't, the grass will and always will.

AUTHOR BIO

Alexander Homoc was born in Melbourne, Australia. He began writing his first novel, Will Ink Suffice, in 2021, when he was 16 years old, and later went on to publish the novel when he was 18, during his final year of senior schooling. Alexander primarily writes literary fiction and poetry, largely focusing on human relationships, love, and tragedy. While writing his first novel, Alexander drew inspiration from his own relationships, using them as a compass, which helped him navigate the characters. Alexander explains that writing provides him with comfort and purpose, especially in a life that can often feel mundane and monotonous. Similar to Vivienne, the protagonist of his debut novel Will Ink Suffice, writing provides solace when the world starts to cave in.

www.ingramcontent.com/pod-product-compliance
Lightning Source LLC
Chambersburg PA
CBHW030914060726
47591CB00005B/1534